A marriage of convenience.

An accepted practice in his time, perhaps, but not in hers. Americans most especially married for love, and only for love. Not for convenience. Not for money. Not for titles or position. And most definitely not to obtain an identity.

Would there be children, Harry wondered.

A better question.

Would there be love?

There was already desire, on his part.

There was already compassion on hers.

Could there be more? Could he believe, trust, in the promise of more?

Dear Reader,

This month, wedding bells ring for six couples who marry for convenient reasons—and discover love by surprise. Join us for their HASTY WEDDINGS.

Kasey Michaels starts off the month with *Timely Matrimony*, a love story with a time-travel twist. It's all in the timing for modern-day bride Suzi Harper, and Harry Wilde, her handsome husband from the nineteenth century. Just as they found happiness, it seemed Harry's destiny was to leave her....

In Anne Peters's *McCullough's Bride*, handsome rancher Nick McCullough rescues single mom Beth Coleman the only way he knows how—he marries her! Now Nick is the one in danger—of losing his heart to a woman who could never return his love.

Popular Desire author Cathie Linz weaves a *One of a Kind Marriage*. In this fast-paced romp, Jenny Benjamin and Rafe Murphy start as enemies, then become man and wife. Marriage may have solved their problems, but can love cure their differences?

The impromptu nuptials continue with *Oh, Baby!*, Lauryn Chandler's humorous look at a single woman who is determined to have a child—and lands herself a husband in the bargain. It's a green card marriage for Kelsey Shepherd and Frankie Falco in *Temporary Groom*. Jayne Addison continues her Falco Family series with this story of short-term commitment—and unending attraction! The laughter continues with Carolyn Zane's *Wife in Name Only*—a tale of marriage—under false pretenses.

I hope you enjoy our HASTY WEDDINGS. In the coming months, look for more books by your favorite authors.

Happy reading,

Anne Canadeo
Senior Editor

Please address questions and book requests to:
Silhouette Reader Service
U.S.: 3010 Walden Ave., P.O. Box 1325, Buffalo, NY 14269
Canadian: P.O. Box 609, Fort Erie, Ont. L2A 5X3

Kasey Michaels

TIMELY MATRIMONY

Silhouette
ROMANCE™
Published by Silhouette Books
America's Publisher of Contemporary Romance

To my niece Lorraine Charles,
because I already dedicated one to her sister,
and because she is as wonderfully "singular" as Suzi.

 SILHOUETTE BOOKS

ISBN 0-373-19030-1

TIMELY MATRIMONY

Copyright © 1994 by Kasey Michaels

This edition published by arrangement with Harlequin Enterprises B. V.

® and TM are trademarks of Harlequin Enterprises B. V., used under
license. Trademarks indicated with ® are registered in the United States
Patent and Trademark Office, the Canadian Trade Marks Office and in
other countries.

Printed in U.S.A.

Books by Kasey Michaels

Silhouette Romance

Maggie's Miscellany #331
Compliments of the Groom #542
Popcorn and Kisses #572
To Marry at Christmas #616
His Chariot Awaits #701
Romeo in the Rain #743
Lion on the Prowl #808
Sydney's Folly #834
Prenuptial Agreement #898
Uncle Daddy #916
Marriage in a Suitcase #949
Timely Matrimony #1030

KASEY MICHAELS,

the author of more than two dozen books, divides her creative time between writing contemporary romance and Regency novels. Married and the mother of four, Kasey's writing has garnered the Romance Writers of America Golden Medallion Award and the *Romantic Times* Best Regency Trophy.

REGENCY RAKE HARRY WILDE'S CHECKLIST FOR THE PERFECT WIFE.

His bride would:

1) Never dance with the same gentleman more than twice in one night.

2) Carefully conceal her ankles when mounting a carriage.

3) Not even think to allow such words as "legs" to pass her unrouged lips.

4) Speak only when spoken to.

5) Never deign to voice an opinion on anything to do with politics or any controversial issue.

6) Defer to her husband in *everything*.

7) Be of a reasonable age—certainly no older than twenty.

And then, Harry Wilde met Suzi Harper....

Prologue

The late-summer storm had been raging for three interminable days and nights, causing the *Pegasus* to be blown badly off course.

But there was nothing anyone on the ship could do, at least not until the storm began to abate. Moment by moment, the *Pegasus* drew closer to the southern New Jersey shoreline, and certain disaster.

Veteran seamen were silent under this threat of imminent death, returning from their exhausting above-deck shifts with pinched gray faces and avoiding the questioning eyes of their mates.

There was no nearby port they could head for, even if they could be assured of a welcome, and everyone knew that if the storm did not ease soon they would be food for the fishes.

And then on the third dawn, just as all seemed lost, the storm disappeared. Not eased, nor merely slowed down, showing signs of soon being over. It simply stopped. One moment the wind had been howling, rain lashing the ship, the sky a dark, menacing gun-metal gray, and the next moment the storm was gone.

The sea, formerly so violent, calmed, and a watery sun began to rise over the horizon. Gulls could be heard screaming as they perched in the rigging, and in the galley men raced to fill their bellies with something other than cold food and stale biscuits.

"I'm going up on deck," Harry announced to his companions, many of whom still suffered from sea-sickness brought on by the roiling waves. He had been stuck belowdecks for what seemed like forever, and the notion of a little fresh air was extremely appealing.

"Don't do it, son," one of the oldest sailors warned as he stuck his unlit pipe into the corner of his mouth. Smoking had been forbidden by the captain until the storm was over, for the last thing the crew of the *Pegasus* needed was a fire on board ship. "I've heard about storms like these. It's not over. This is only the eye."

Harry smiled, pushing a stray lock of longish blond hair back off his forehead. "The eye, is it? Fascinating. Well then, my fainthearted friend, I think I shall go 'eye' it."

"Be careful," the seaman cautioned. "We've got men climbing all over the riggings. It's plenty danger-ous up there, especially for a wobbly-legs like you."

"It's prodigiously dangerous down here, my good fellow," Harry countered, picking up his pouch and slinging its heavy leather strap over his head—he went nowhere without his pouch. "One more moment looking at your hangdog face and I might weep. Don't worry. I'll be back in a minute.''

So saying, he bounded up the short, steep flight of steps and opened the hatch, the fresh sea air teasing his senses so that he hurriedly scrambled onto the deck and headed for the railing, intent on catching his first glimpse of the New Jersey shoreline as the land was lit by the rising sun.

How flat it all was, covered only by shrub, so that he could see that they were lying close beside an island, with the true shoreline, and what appeared to be an immense forest of pines behind it.

The breaker island, as he supposed such an area of land was called, was ringed by a wide, unbroken stretch of white sand and populated by thousands upon thousands of gulls, all of them screaming—and some of them laughing, Harry thought—as they plundered the wet sand for the treasure trove of small sea creatures that has been washed there by the storm.

It was a beautiful, inspiring scene, with the sky the clearest blue Harry could remember, and the sun glowing red from behind him, turning the ocean into a vast fairyland of shining lights.

Harry was mesmerized by the sight in front of him, his romantic soul enlivened by nature's display of grandeur, his full attention on the shoreline, and not on the men climbing overhead in the riggings, doing their best to make repairs on the mizzenmast.

"Avast aft! *Avast*, man!"

What the devil? Aft? Which way was aft? Harry had been aboard the *Pegasus* for over two months, but he'd be damned for a tinker if he'd figured out fore and aft, or port and starboard for that matter.

He wasn't a sailor; had no notion of becoming a sailor. He was only on board this ship because it was the right thing to do, the right place to be. His heart certainly wasn't in it. Only his body.

"Aft?" he yelled, wheeling around and looking heavenward just in time for the broken piece of rigging to deal him a glancing blow on the temple. It wasn't enough to kill him outright, but did serve to turn the sunny morning into darkest night as he pitched backward and tumbled, unknowing, into the sunlit sea.

Chapter One

Click. "—said to the gorilla, 'I don't know. We don't serve *ducks!*' *Beep! Beep!* Yes, indeedy, folks. Another two beeper. Too bad, Maisie from Cape May. It takes four beeps," *Beep! Beep! Beep! Beep!* "of the old car horn to make your joke eligible for our weekly drawing. So this is Annoying Arnie in the A.M. reminding you early birds out there to keep those jokes and limericks coming. The prize this week is a full, six-piece set of steak knives, compliments of WLFJ and—"

Suzi Harper frantically beat on the top of her clock-radio with both hands until she located the snooze-alarm bar and silenced the screaming Arnie. Then she fell back against the pillows, breathing heavily as she glared up at the ceiling fan above her bed.

She must have been farther out of her mind than usual. Setting her alarm for five-thirty could be nothing less than proof of an impending mental breakdown, most probably brought on by the three-day-long storm that had kept her cooped up inside her Ocean City condo.

Why else would she think it such a splendid idea if she were to rise before dawn to search the beach outside for pieces of driftwood for Mrs. O'Connell?

She closed her eyes, sighing. Poor Mrs. O'Connell. The woman had looked so pitiful the other day when she showed Suzi her collection of driftwood art—if anyone could call bits of wood stuck all over with plastic flowers and seashells *art*.

But Mrs. O'Connell, Suzi's closest neighbor, obviously delighted in the pastime, and her complaint that her arthritis kept her from combing the beach for "exquisite" pieces of driftwood after a storm before the morning beach patrol swept the area had touched Suzi's soft heart.

"And my even softer head," Suzi grumbled tiredly, throwing back the covers. "Next time I make someone a promise, first I'll be sure it has nothing to do with getting up in the middle of the night."

She glowered at the clock-radio as she turned off the alarm. All she needed now was for the snooze bar to pop again and hear Annoying Arnie's ridiculously cheerful, adenoidal tones reminding her that it was now only five thirty-*five* in the "A.M."

She slid her ruby red painted toes off the bed and onto the woven grass mat Wilbur Langley had brought her back from his last trip to Tahiti and dropped her head into her hands, pushing equally ruby red tipped fingers into her chin-length ash blond hair.

"C'mon, Harper, you can do this. Just get with the program," she admonished herself as she stood, doing her best to open her eyes and focus them on the brightening dawn just outside her window.

Except all the vertical blinds were still tightly shut against the scary streaks of lightning that had kept her awake past two o'clock last night, so that she couldn't see much of anything.

Padding to the window while clad only in an emerald green silk camisole and matching tap pants, and yawning prodigiously as she went, she pushed back the blinds and blinked several times as the rising sun cut through the morning mist, giving her a dose of brightness she hadn't expected.

"At least the storm's finally blown over," she said to Patchwork, her five-year-old calico cat, who was still blissfully, annoyingly asleep at the bottom of the queen-size bed. "And sure enough, there's the driftwood, just like Mrs. O'Connell promised. Driftwood, and a helmet crab—ugh, without the crab, and—" she wrinkled her small pert nose, "—sixteen tons of sickening, slimy, mussel-stuffed seaweed. Oh, joy."

She was just about to turn away from the window when something else on the beach, something just at the water's edge, caught her eye. Too big to be driftwood, too solid to be seaweed, it resembled... "*A man!* Dear Lord. Patchwork—it's a *man!*"

Call 911, call 911, her brain screamed to her as she ran out of the ground-floor bedroom and raced toward the spiral staircase that would take her upstairs, to the telephone in the kitchen.

She had her foot on the second step from the top before she remembered that she hadn't had the phone hooked up. For the month she had planned to spend in Ocean City, a total disconnect with modern communication seemed to be a good idea—or at least had at the time.

It figured. Every stupid thing she'd ever done in all of her thirty-two years had seemed to be a good idea at the time.

Suzi retraced her steps and fumbled with the dead bolt. Throwing open the door at the side of the condo, she sprinted toward the beach, her bare feet slapping against the cold, hard, wet sand.

The sun was just creeping above the horizon, turning the sea to gold, and she had no difficulty in making out the location of the man's body as it lay half in, half out of the water.

Not his body, you idiot! she admonished herself as she ran, forgetful of the fact that she was still in her nightclothes. Her fairly skimpy, revealing nightclothes. *He's not dead. Please, don't let him be dead. What on earth would I do with a dead body? Decorate it with plastic flowers and seashells?*

Breathless, she dropped to her knees on the sand, beside the man. He was lying on his stomach, his hands beside his head, his long legs at the mercy of the still angry waves that broke farther out on the beach, then foamed up onto the shore.

He wasn't moving—unless she counted his legs, which were almost floating. His face, the small bit of it she could see, was a ghastly gray beneath his dark blond hair. She took only a moment to consider the man's unusual dress.

His woolen pants, shrunk up to just below his knees by the seawater, and his white shirt, its long, full sleeves plastered against his arms, were not exactly the usual outfit of vacationers.

"Oh, who cares, Suzi? This is no time to play fashion police!" she berated herself, pushing both hands against one of the man's shoulders and heaving him over onto his side. It wasn't an easy job, for he was tall, and rather muscular, his body heavy with seawater and the sand that caked him head to toe, but at last she managed it.

"Ugh. He's dead, all right," she said, sitting back on her haunches, shivering and shaking her hands to rid them of the feel of his solid, cold body. "Real dead. Real, *real* dead."

But then, as Suzi was not the sort to give in gracefully, she took a deep breath and narrowed her eyes, her small, fairly belligerent chin lifting a notch as she decided that she hadn't raced outside in her camisole to give up without one hell of a fight.

She laced her fingers together tightly, almost as if in prayer, trying desperately to recall the public service program she had seen recently on cardiopulmonary resuscitation. Then she decided she remembered at least *some* of it.

First she should give him a good crack between the shoulder blades, just to let him know she was there. That seemed reasonable—or was that what she should do to a choking victim? No. That was what people *used* to do to choking victims. Now they performed that squeezing thing called the Heimlich maneuver.

Well, too bad. She'd already hit him. She'd hit him once, then twice, just for good measure. It had been like hitting lead. Cold, solid lead.

Then, her hands shaking violently, she pushed him all the way over onto his back and, while prudently looking the other way, cautiously stuck one finger in his mouth, believing she should check to make sure his windpipe wasn't obstructed.

Stupid rule, she thought, her finger scraping against the man's upper teeth. *It isn't like he's got a herring stuck down his gullet or anything.*

Only once she was satisfied that she'd followed all the instructions she'd seen in the public service program did she pull at the strap of the leather pouch the man had draped over his shoulders and throw the thing onto the sand. Then she began tearing at the buttons on his shirt, revealing his broad, slightly golden chest.

Golden? she thought, belatedly realizing that his entire chest, now exposed to the sunlight, was covered with a blond down that, although crusted with sand, was soft to the touch.

"That's the ticket, Suzi, waste precious time admiring the guy, why don't you," she told herself, knowing she was speaking aloud so that the only sounds coming to her ears were not those of the waves and her own rapidly beating heart. "Go to it!"

After giving herself that order she straddled the man at his waist, hating the feel of his cold wet clothing against the inside of her thighs.

Placing her hands on his chest just below his neck, she measured down three handspans until she believed she had found the correct spot, then laid one hand on top of the other and pressed down—hard.

Going up on her haunches in order to gain leverage, she repeated the movement, counting aloud for five beats, then leaned forward and, holding his nostrils pinched, puffed into his mouth five times.

She didn't know if five was the correct number, or if she was in danger of killing the dead man —*how do you kill a dead man?*—but at least she was doing something, which had to be a whacking lot better than doing nothing.

Alternating the puffs with the chest compressions, Suzi worked for what seemed like forever, although she hadn't been performing her peculiar version of CPR for more than a few minutes the man suddenly coughed, then moved his arms.

"Yes!" Suzi screamed, slapping his face as she bounced lightly on his pelvis, caught between exhaustion and an exhilaration close to euphoria. "That's it, mister—breathe. *Breathe!*"

Eyes the color of the ocean at dawn opened wide and looked straight up at her for a moment before he unceremoniously pushed her away, turned onto his side, and began to retch violently onto the sand.

He was sick for some moments, which didn't bother Suzi, who was busy jumping up and down on the sand, offering high fives to any imaginary onlookers who might be applauding her performance.

She had done it! She—silly, flighty, airheaded Suzanne Harper—was an official, bona fide, card-carrying *heroine*.

Who said she was only good enough to write book reviews and look good while dangling from some man's arm at trendy Manhatten cocktail parties? She was *woman,* damn it—and she had just saved a man's life.

She stopped jumping up and down, remembering that the man was far from saved. He was still lying on the beach, and he was still, she noticed, looking as pale as the underbelly of a fish. Now she knew where that expression had come from, she thought randomly as she dropped to her knees in the sand and looked at her patient.

"Are you all right now?" she asked, ducking her head so that she could see beneath the hair that was hanging in his face, nearly obscuring his features. "I mean, do you think you're done being sick?"

He collapsed onto his back and raised one arm to shield his eyes from the sun. "Ow!" he said immediately, then gingerly touched a hand to his temple. "That's quite a lump. What happened?"

"You're asking *me?*" Suzi scrambled to her feet, holding out a hand to help him rise. He stood slowly, leaning heavily against her, one arm around her shoulders.

Her knees nearly buckled under his weight. "Hey, who do I look like, Superwoman? Come on. My house is right here. Try to help yourself a little bit, okay? You've got to be over six feet tall, and I'm a full foot shorter, and about one hundred and twenty pounds lighter—and that's not counting the fact that you're sopping wet and piled with sand."

He took a single step away from the beach.

"Well," she said, grimacing, "it's a start. Look, I could leave you here and go call the authorities. The tide's going out, so you'd be in no danger of washing out to sea again. Maybe that would be better."

Suddenly the man showed her a strength she hadn't supposed possible. "No. Not the authorities. I'll be all right, I assure you. Just let me hold on to you. I can make it."

"Great, now he thinks *he's* Superman!" Suzi mumbled, helping him as slowly, one small step at a time, they made their way back up the beach and onto the path leading to the condo.

They entered through the still-open door and Suzi steered him toward her bedroom, which was the only way she could steer him. She had learned as they made their way up the beach that he was like every grocery store shopping cart she had ever used—he might be capable of forward movement, but he could only make right turns.

Using her last possible burst of energy she propelled him toward the unmade bed, where he collapsed onto his back, immediately making a soggy mess of her freshly laundered sheets.

Patchwork, highly put out to see she had a bedmate, hopped down and exited the room, tail held high.

"Am I in heaven?" the man asked almost reverently as he looked up at her.

"Right," she answered curtly, sinking to the floor, her chest still heaving with her exertions of the past ten minutes. "And I'm the angel Gabriel. Don't worry, you're not dead. You just feel like you ought to be. So do I. I should get ten merit badges for this one! Now just let me catch my breath and I'll go call for help."

"No!" he commanded tersely, although his eyes were closed, as if he was too weary to keep them open. And his voice did have an unmistakable note of command, especially for somebody who, at the moment at least, most closely resembled a drowned rat. "You'll be well rewarded for your assistance—as well as your silence."

Her silence? She wasn't going to call Annoying Arnie and have it put out over the airwaves for a set of steak knives. All she wanted to do was call for help. What was with this guy, anyway?

"Look, mister, you've been injured. You've got a lump on the side of your head I could hang my hat on. You have a concussion, at the least, and might even have a fractured skull, which can be very dangerous. I'm no doctor, so it only makes sense for me to—"

"Stifle yourself! Good Lord, woman, is your tongue hinged at both ends?" he interrupted, frowning fiercely, then touched his chest, his neck, obviously searching for something. "My pouch. What have you done with my pouch, madam?" he asked a moment later, struggling to rise. "I must have my pouch!"

She wanted to kill him. She should be allowed to do that. It only seemed fair. After all, she had been the one who had saved him. Her tongue hinged at both ends, indeed. Who did this guy think he was—Wilbur?

"It's still on the beach," she told him, taking some small pleasure in the notion that her news wouldn't please him.

He turned his head to look at her, darn near pinning her to the floor with the heat of his gaze, then raised his hand to his temple and closed his eyes once more. "What is it doing there? Why did you leave it? Fetch it to me at once!"

"Fetch it yourself, bucko. I gave at the office," Suzi responded, rising to begin brushing the sand off her arms, her bare thighs. Damn, couldn't the guy at least say thank you?

What was in that pouch, anyway, his life savings? The man should be down on his knees, kissing her feet, grateful to be alive. "I'm going to take a quick shower in the guest bathroom, then call someone to take you away. You should have a doctor look at that bump on your head."

"Get me my pouch, woman!"

"Hey, now look—" Suzi began angrily, jamming her hands down on her hips. Then he opened his eyes once more, those gorgeous, black-lashed, heavenly blue-green eyes, and she knew she was beaten.

As she watched, he struggled to rise, only to fall back onto the pillows once more, exhausted. "Oh, what the hell," she said, shaking her head. "All right, I'll go get the thing. What's in it, anyway? And it better not be drugs!"

"Drugs? What would I do with drugs? I'm not an apothecary. It's my—my manuscript," he answered, curling his long body against the mattress. "Just fetch it. Please. And then let me rest here for a moment. Only for a while. Then I'll be on my way. I—I won't be any trouble. Any trouble at all."

"It's too late for that promise," Suzi told him, but he was asleep, his chest rising and falling rhythmically, his color already much improved.

She really should call the police, or at least go next door and phone for an ambulance. A couple of paramedics might come in handy. Yes, that's what she should do. Call for help. Lots of help.

But, as she retrieved the pouch from the beach— and picked up a couple of pieces of interesting looking driftwood for Mrs. O'Connell while she was at it— Suzi thought once more about the man's strange clothes, and his decidedly British accent. There was something very strange, and very strangely exciting about this whole business.

Maybe she should wait. After all, he was in no condition to hurt her. He couldn't lick his weight in sand flies at the moment.

She'd just take that shower she'd mentioned, brew a pot of coffee, and take a look at the guy's manuscript. A writer? Had he faked this whole thing so that she'd look at his work and maybe put in a good word with Wilbur or some other publisher?

It seemed like a pretty desperate act, but just look at that guy who had threatened to fly his private plane into one publisher's office a dozen or so years back. Stranger things had happened.

But a drowned man landing on her beach with his manuscript conveniently strapped to his body? It was just too farfetched. Nobody would believe it.

"Yes, they would, Suzie," she told herself as she dropped the pouch on the foyer floor and headed for the bathroom. "That's the great pity of the thing. You're *just* the sort of person these crazy things happen to—and it's beginning to get pretty darn boring!"

Chapter Two

Harry woke to the aroma of freshly brewed coffee, immediately aware that his stomach was empty and he was more than a little hungry.

He had barely eaten anything during the course of the storm, especially once the cook had slipped in the galley and broken his leg as the ship pitched in response to one of the larger waves.

The cook had spilled the pot of soup as he'd grabbed for a handhold as he went down, too, which had been a damnable shame, for that soup had been intended for their supper.

But the sea was calm now, so the storm must be over at last, and none too soon.

He moved his legs tentatively, realizing that he was on a bed and not lying in the too-short hammock that had been his berth on the *Pegasus* for two months. He must be in the captain's cabin, although how he had come to be there he had no idea.

Yes, yes, he did. He had gone above decks, to take a look at the coastline. He remembered that. He also remembered someone calling a warning to him, and then—and then?

Harry frowned, the action immediately sending a wicked pain through his skull. He lifted one hand to his temple and felt the lump that was just in front of his hairline.

That was it! He'd taken a whack to the noggin—a bruising blow, if he was to be considered any judge in the matter—and toppled overboard. Now, after being fished out of the sea, he was tucked up in the captain's cabin, recuperating.

But he was still all wet, even though someone had thought to throw a blanket over him. Ah, well. At least he was out of that miserable hammock.

He shifted slightly on the mattress, enjoying the decadence of crisp, clean, sweet-smelling sheets, then slowly forced open his eyes, intending to take an assessing look at the lap of luxury he'd just landed in.

"Bloody hell," he said a moment later, staring up at the circle of sharp metal blades hanging against the ceiling. What sort of ridiculous invention was that?

He turned his head to the left, to see that he was in a very large room—too large to be a ship's cabin— and it was filled with delicate white furnishings he immediately identified as being of Imperial French design.

French? Where the devil was he? And this wasn't just any room. It was a lady's bedchamber; he was convinced of it.

He turned to his right, his heart beginning to beat rapidly, and saw wedges of light coming through strange, narrow shutters, then blinked twice as he saw the painting on the wall directly across from the bed.

It was an enormous portrait of a young woman, a rather ethereally beautiful young woman who had been painted as she half reclined on some large boulders close by the sea, her hands braced behind her, her blond hair blowing in the breeze.

She looked like a fairy sprite, her pink-and-white flowered gown just skimming the tops of her bare feet, a large straw hat decorated with roses lying beside her on the rocks.

But it was her face that struck him, jabbing at his brain, mocking him with her laughing blue eyes.

Am I in heaven?

Right. And I'm the angel Gabriel.

"Bloody hell!" Harry exclaimed again, bolting upright, a reckless move that sent all the bells of Westminster Abbey to mercilessly clanging in his head at one time.

"Oh, good, you're awake. You've been sleeping for hours. I thought the smell of my special coffee might do the trick, although I think you should hop in the shower before you eat. Those wool slacks are beginning to smell. I'll probably have to buy a new mattress, but I suppose that's a small price to pay for being a heroine. Here, I ran out to one of the boardwalk shops that opens at eight-thirty and picked up some clothes for you. Even underwear. Your clothes are past saving, you know. The guest bathroom is that way, on the other side of the foyer.''

She stopped talking for a moment, most probably to catch her breath. ''Oh, and by the way, I'm Suzanne Harper, although I suppose you can call me Suzi, seeing as how you've been sleeping in my bed.''

If the portrait hadn't jogged Harry's memory, the young woman's propensity for long-winded speeches would have served his purposes just as well.

She was dressed very informally in a vibrantly striped green-and-white dressing gown of some nubby material, her hair tied up on her head with an emerald green ribbon, her feet barely covered by strange, thonglike slippers.

She had worn green before, on the beach, although he seemed to remember that she had been nearly naked, her long, straight legs visible for his inspection— not that he had been in any mood for seduction.

''You—you're the one who pulled me out of the sea, aren't you? I remember now. No one on the ship rescued me. You did. And you're an American, of course. I can tell by your accent. Where are we? Who holds control of this stretch of land—you, or us? Silly question. We don't control much of anything anymore, at least not below Canada. Not since that debacle at York. Have you rescued me simply to turn me over to your soldiers?''

''Oh, good. Oh, yes, this is good. This is just great,'' the woman who had introduced herself as Suzi said, backing toward the door, her hands held out in front of her as if preparing to ward him off if he should attack. "I've rescued a nut case! Why me? Why is it always me? Why not? Why should this time be different?"

She halted beside the open door and picked up a strange-looking bag, tossing it to him so that he instinctively caught it, then set it aside.

"Now listen, fella. I'm not looking for trouble. Here's your clothes. Just put them on and get out of here. Your pouch is on the foyer floor. I didn't even open it, promise! I'll be out on the beach—me *and* my purse—counting to one thousand. If you're not gone by then, I'm sending for the cavalry. You got that?"

"Wait!" Harry called out as she turned to make her escape—as if he was going to hurt her or something. He had to say something. Something that would make her stay. Something that would convince her that he meant no harm. If he left the safety of her house now, without any preparation, he'd be in an American prison before nightfall.

"I haven't thanked you yet, Miss Harper," he went on, deciding he'd attempt to be charming, which wasn't easy, for he felt like death. "You did a brave thing, rescuing a drowning man. You have my eternal gratitude."

"Well, I should most certainly hope so!" Suzi declared, turning back to look at him once more. He grinned, knowing his smile was rather endearing—or so many women had told him—and watched as she relaxed her guard slightly. "You know, I thought you were dead. But that CPR stuff is really something else. I'm rather proud of myself, actually."

"CPR? And what, Miss Harper, is CPR?"

"Oh, never mind. Um—look. You had quite a knock on the head, and I shouldn't be surprised if your brains are a little scrambled. Just forget what I said a moment ago. Take your time. Have your shower while I see about getting you something to eat. Use my bathroom—it's just through that door over there. Then you can be on your way. All right?"

Harry shoved back the constricting blanket, levered his legs over the edge of the bed and pushed himself to his feet. He had gone up on deck sans his boots and must have lost his stockings in the water, so that his legs were bare to the hem of his breeches.

Even his shirt had been torn open, so that he drew the edges of cloth together over his chest, doing his best to make a decent, nonthreatening appearance. After all, he still had quite a headache, and he didn't want to set her off again.

Not that hers wasn't a pleasant voice. He just didn't need to hear her talk so much—although he didn't mind looking at her. It had been well over two months since he'd been in the company of a beautiful woman.

"Thank you once more, Miss Harper," he drawled in his most congenial tone, pushing a hand through his drying, sea-salt sticky hair. "And perhaps you might be persuaded to have one of your servants draw me a tub as well. If it wouldn't be too much trouble, that is."

He watched, amazed, as her eyes nearly popped out of her head. "Servants? Draw you a *tub?*" She seemed to lose any fear she might have of him as she advanced once more into the room, shaking a finger at him—a finger painted a bright, vulgar red very much in contrast to her petite, blond beauty.

Had he ended up in the household of a well-financed courtesan? And, was that so bad? He could have washed up in front of a bear cave or something.

"Now look, mister," she continued heatedly, "fun's fun and all that, and I suppose you've got some sort of lingering concussion or something, but it's time to give it a rest. You're not in jolly old England now."

"I know," he answered, liking the way she challenged him, either unaware or uncaring of the fact that he was so much larger and stronger than she, and capable of silencing her with one hand. "I'm in America and, since you were the one to discover me, your prisoner, I suppose."

"My prisoner?" Suzie asked him, frowning, her arm dropping to her side. "My prisoner of *what,* for crying out loud?"

And she questioned *his* sanity? "Your prisoner of war, of course, madam. You have heard that we just recently captured one of your frigates, haven't you? I believe it was called the *Chesapeake.*"

"Uh-huh," Suzi mumbled, beginning to back toward the doorway once more. "The *Chesapeake.* That would be during the War of 1812, I believe, having just reviewed a really *dreadful* book on the subject. I gave it a scathing critique, too, now that I recall. Just because it's history, it doesn't have to be unremittingly boring, you know. I think I'm beginning to understand now. This is all some sort of twisted joke, isn't it? You wouldn't happen to be Professor Jonathan Blakeheart, would you? I mean, I've heard of some really rotten stunts being pulled by authors who got their noses in a snit because of a bad review, but—''

''You do enjoy listening to the sound of your own voice, don't you?'' Harry offered affably, slowly advancing toward her. ''And a most lovely voice it is, too, not that I understand half of what you're saying. My name is Harry. Harry Wilde. Of Sussex. I'm a writer of sorts, even a historian, but most certainly not a professor. At the moment, however, I am a soldier, and your prisoner.''

''Uh-huh,'' she said again, her monosyllabic answers beginning to tear at his nerves even more than her earlier marathon speeches.

''Yes, well, I shan't be boring, shall I? But what's this about a war of 1812, Miss Harper? You speak as if it's already concluded. This is 1813, and we're still engaged in hostilities, although I don't believe either side has ever really had its heart in the thing. We English have enough on our plate with Napoléon still running about Europe unchecked.''

''1813,'' she repeated, picking up a hairbrush and brandishing it in front of her like a weapon. ''Uh-huh. Sure it is—if you say so. And Napoléon, too. That's good, very good, tossing old Boney in there for good measure. I'm impressed. Really. Although I thought you people all believed *you* were Napoléon. Go on, Professor Blakeheart. Tell me more. I'm all ears!''

She was looking at him as if convinced he was mad—or some sort of impostor—a circumstance that was beginning to make him angry.

''Yes, and very lovely ears they are, although I don't believe there's anything of any great import between them," he countered, wishing he still didn't feel so damnably weak. "What's the matter with you, woman? It's 1813, just in the first days of August, although I've rather lost track these past few days, what with the storm raging about our heads and all. I'm English, you're an American—and our two countries are at war."

"At war. America and England. Uh-huh," Suzi said again in that maddening singsong way he'd heard employed on children telling their elders whopping great fibs about ghosties and dragons they'd espied out under their beds in the middle of the night. She pointed toward the corner of the room and a strange, glass-fronted box that sat on a white pedestal. "And what's that?"

"What is what? That?" Harry shrugged, unable to understand her point. "That, Miss Harper, is some sort of box. A container for your personal belongings, perhaps? And enormously ugly, if you really desire my opinion. It clashes badly with the remainder of the room. Madam, what *are* you about?"

"It's a television set, you idiot—a *television*— and don't you go telling me it's a box!" Suzi all but screamed at him. "Just watch, as if you don't already know what's going to happen," she demanded, still brandishing the hairbrush as she skipped across the room, picked up a much smaller black box, this one in the shape of a flattened rectangle, and aimed it at the larger box. He heard a small *click*.

Harry flinched, expecting an imminent explosion, then looked, startled, as the larger box seemed to come to life, a colorful drawing appearing inside it. The drawing resembled a sailor, although he barely seemed human.

"I'm Popeye the sailor man," the drawing sang, swinging its large, grotesquely out of proportion arms, "I'm Popeye the sailor man—"

There was another slight *click* and the large box seemed to flicker once more, then go dark.

"All right, buster," Suzi challenged, stepping into his line of sight, blocking out the box. "I've got you now. So, tell me again. Is it 1813?"

"God's teeth, what a fascinating trick!" Harry, truly impressed, unceremoniously pushed her to one side and dropped to his knees in front of the box, placing his hands against the cool, dark glass.

"Where did he go?" he asked, turning to look at her, not sure if he should be frightened or impressed with this show of American ingenuity that was so much advanced of English shadowboxes, which were small, and handheld, and not nearly so clever. "What did you do with the sailor? And how did you make him talk?"

"You—you don't know?" The small rectangular box dropped to the floor. "No, of course you don't. Nobody could be such a good actor—especially not a professor. And you don't know what a shower is, do you? That's why you asked me to have a servant draw you a tub. Oh, you poor man. You need a doctor! You—you really do think this is 1813. Don't you?"

"Of course I do, because it *is*. It's 1813, and I just fell overboard from my ship after a storm. I say, Miss Harper, is there anyone else about I might speak with? Someone in authority? Your nurse—your *keeper?*"

Harry said, then sat back on his heels and looked at her levelly, immediatey sorry he had insulted her. She didn't look too well all of a sudden; her cheeks were pale and her lovely blue eyes very wide. "Miss Harper? Are you all right?"

"He thinks it's 1813," Suzi said, as if to herself. "He doesn't *look* crazy. But he *has* to be crazy. Because if he's not . . . if he's *not,* then he really *is* from . . . but now he's *here* . . . and I'll have to tell him where he is . . . *when* he is—and—oh, dear Lord!"

She seemed to sway where she stood, so that Harry went to her quickly, taking hold of her upper arms just as her eyes rolled up in her head and she fell forward against his chest.

Chapter Three

Suzi came awake all at once, instantly realizing that she was lying on damp sheets.

What had happened to her? Had she fainted? Well, of course she had fainted! Who wouldn't faint when presented with the theory that the man she had saved from drowning was actually some sort of time traveller? Fainting was the least she should have done, with screaming and then running for her life still a viable second option.

"Ugh!" she protested, rolling onto her side, feeling the room spinning around her.

"Lie still, woman, or else you'll swoon again," Harry warned from somewhere above her. "I have enough on my plate as it is without that."

"Harry? You're still here?" Suzi asked, opening her eyes to see the handsome blond Englishman sitting on the edge of the bed. "I—I had rather hoped this was all some sort of nightmare and you'd be gone. But I should have known better. I wouldn't be that lucky.''

She motioned for him to move aside and sat up, looking straight at him. ''Sorry I fainted. I'm not usually that sort, which is a pity because, if I could learn to swoon at will I could get myself out of some boring parties a lot easier.''

Realizing she was babbling—something he obviously did not like, she shut up, remembering that she had something extremely important to tell him. But how?

''Harry?'' she nervously ventured at last, deliberately avoiding his eyes. ''Um, Mr. Wilde—there's something I have to tell you. Something I don't think you're going to want to hear. You see, although at first I thought you were pulling my leg, and then I thought maybe you were just rowing without both oars in the water, now I think that maybe, that just *maybe*—''

''I already know, Miss Harper,'' he interrupted her, so that she looked at him curiously.

''You already know? You already know what?''

''I know that this isn't 1813,'' he answered, running his fingers through his hair. His strong, well-shaped fingers. His romantically long dark blond hair. His wonderfully made body. His extremely handsome, appealing face.

Good Lord, Harper, what are you thinking? Are you out of your tiny mind? He's still all wet and caked with sand. And he's alone with you in your bedroom! Get up! Get out of this room before something terrible happens!

"How—how do you know that?" she asked, suddenly glad she had put her beach wrapper on over her bikini in order to go up on the boardwalk to buy her time traveler some underwear.

She couldn't imagine what might have happened—what sort of shock she might have placed on his nineteenth-century system—if she had walked into the room half-naked.

As it was, he probably thought she was a streetwalker, or a loose woman, or a camp follower, or whatever it was they called prostitutes in Regency England.

And so what if he did? It wasn't as if he'd be interested in her romantically. She was thirty-two years old, young by her standards, but positively ancient to a man who came from a society where any woman over the age of twenty-one was considered an old maid without a prayer of marriage. He was thirty-five if he was a day, and just right for her, age-wise—not that he'd think so.

Right for me? What am I thinking? Did I faint, or have some sort of mental collapse?

"Harry?" she repeated shakily when he didn't answer her question, but just sat there, fondling her remote control. "*How* you do know?"

"How? It's rather obvious, don't you think? Your very different-looking house, that box with the sailor inside it? I've never seen anything like either of them. You Americans might be inventive, but you aren't that much ahead of us. But, to be truthful, I used this," he said, holding up the remote control.

"You turned on the television? I'll bet that was a shock," Suzi inserted, giggling nervously and wondering if she shouldn't faint again. It seemed a reasonable alternative to what was taking place at the moment in her bedroom.

"Yes, it was, rather. I pushed the button labeled Power which seemed a logical choice, then a few other buttons, and a man inside that box over there told me. You called it a tele-vision machine? Interesting use of the language, I suppose. I don't know where the sailor man went. But it's not 1813. It's 1994."

Suzi rolled her eyes, wondering if, since it didn't seem as if she could faint, she might give some serious thought to taking up drinking. "Oh, brother, Harry. You *do* know."

"Yes, Miss Harper, although I don't quite understand the expression, I agree. *Oh, brother.*" He looked at her and laughed, rather endearingly, she decided.

"And it's August 4, 1994, to be precise about the thing," he told her incredulously. "The temperature at the Atlantic City Airport—he did say airport, I'm sure of that, not *sea*port, so I imagine you Americans have mastered balloon flight, which was little more than a hobby in my day—is currently eighty-one degrees, the winds are out of the southwest at two knots and high tide is scheduled for three o'clock this afternoon. And, oh yes, there will be a buffet dinner tonight at an establishment called Jocelyn's, with all you can eat for a single price. Do you like shrimp? We'd have to peel it ourselves, but, I suppose that's a reasonable concession, considering we can eat until we're bilious."

"Oh, Harry, you poor man!" Suzi took hold of his arm, hurting for him. "You're frightened, aren't you?" she asked, knowing she would not be behaving half so well if she had been put into his position. Not her. She'd be racing around the room, crying for her mother! "Are you going to be all right?"

He placed a hand over hers. "I'll be fine, Miss Harper—Suzi. Just fine. I think."

He scratched his upper arm. "Although I still would like that tub. I'm beginning to offend myself, and I ache all over, as if I tumbled head over heels along the sea floor all the way from 1813. God's teeth, do you hear me? I should, by all rights, be dead. But I'm not. I'm alive, and I'm in 1994! What a grand adventure! It's astounding. Simply astounding!"

Oh, he was cool, Harry Wilde was, Suzi decided. A real stiff-upper-lip Englishman and all that sort of rot. But he had to be dying inside, just *dying!*

"Pick up that bag and follow me," she told him, scooting off the bed and heading for her bathroom. "If you think the television machine is something, you're going to *love* my shower massage attachment!"

In the end, Suzi had to turn on the shower for him, adjust the temperature and then, after removing the tags from Harry's new clothes, stand outside the door, waiting for him to finish.

That took some time, and probably most of her hot water, so that she decided against another shower herself and hid in her walk-in closet while she stripped out of her bikini.

She then dived into underwear and the single dress she had brought with her from Manhattan, and was back standing in front of the closed bathroom door a good five minutes before Harry popped his head out.

His hair was still wet, although he had brushed it back from his forehead, its length nothing out of the ordinary, thanks to current styles.

And he was smiling again, so that she could smell her minty toothpaste on his breath. She always kept a supply of guest toothbrushes at the condo, because friends who visited her from New York rarely arrived with them. She had decided it had something to do with living in the center of the world, where everything from antipasto to ironing boards was readily available from room service.

"So that's a shower, Miss Harper? Outstanding! Really. One minute it's there, warm and wet, and with the push of a knob—presto!—it's gone. I'm extremely impressed. However, grateful as I am for all your kindnesses, I don't believe I can wear these— these articles of *clothing* you've purchased."

"Why not?" Suzi inquired blankly.

He sighed, rolling his eyes, then stepped out into the bedroom and turned in a full circle in front of her.

His long, straight, golden hair-dusted legs and really A-1 rear end certainly did justice to the white duck shorts, and the navy blue muscle shirt bearing the words It's Better in Ocean City showed off his slim waist and broad shoulders—not to mention his blond hair—to advantage.

In short, Harry Wilde was a hunk, no matter what century he'd hailed from.

"So?" Suzi asked, wincing as she heard the nervous squeak in her voice. "Where's the problem?"

"Don't be obtuse, Miss Harper." Harry bit out the words, once more rubbing the bruise at his temple. "I saw the man in the box—in the tele-vision machine. He wasn't outfitted in such a ramshackle manner. He had on a shirt, a jacket and some odd sort of wildly dotted neck cloth. It wasn't precisely like that of the Four Horse Club, but then I've always thought that outfit and the membership in general, to be a trifle overdone. In any event, he didn't look anything like this."

"Oh, good. The man's a prude," Suzi said, wrinkling her nose.

"And what's this?" he went on, pulling at the white, ironed-on print on the front of his shirt. "*What's* better in Ocean City? And where—I must add—is Ocean City? Why would anyone call a city after an ocean? Seems to smack of a lack of imagination, don't you think?"

"*This* is Ocean City, Harry," she answered, beginning to see the humor in the thing, "and I suppose you're right. The founding fathers could have called it Stratford-on-Atlantic, or something equally romantic. And I'm sorry about the shirt."

She imagined he had never come across T-shirt advertising and manufacturer's logos on clothing from his time. Beau Brummell, she was convinced, would never have approved. "Everyone wears shirts like that while they're on vacation." She giggled as he rolled his eyes in exasperation. "Just be happy I didn't get you one of the raunchier ones."

"Go on, Miss Harper. Indulge yourself to the top of your bent at my expense. Enjoy yourself. You may believe it is acceptable to parade about with news-print all over you, and showing your limbs to all and sundry, but *I* do not."

"Yup. A prude."

"Don't look down your nose at me, madam. I don't wish to call attention to myself, reveal my dilemma, until I have sufficient time to take stock of my situation, as—priding myself in the notion that the countryside isn't littered with century-hopping En-glishmen—I have no wish to become some sort of sci-entific oddity. Therefore, I suggest you go out to these shops you mentioned once more, and this time return with something more suitable."

"If you go out on the beach in a business suit you might as well set off a few flares as well, shouting to everyone that you're out of place. And, Harry, you really do have to stop ordering me around. It's begin-ning to wear thin, okay?"

His smile turned her knees to water.

"Look," Suzi ended quickly, pushing him toward the spiral staircase in the foyer, "I know this is diffi-cult to understand, but Ocean City is a resort, and people come here because they don't have to wear suits or ties—outfits and neck cloths to you."

She led him upstairs and pointed toward the living room, which she had only recently redecorated in lovely eighteenth-century reproductions, which should have made him feel somewhat at home.

"Open the door that leads onto the deck—um, the porch? The balcony? The portico?" she instructed, madly groping for the correct term. "And I'll join you outside in a moment with our coffee. While you're waiting, take a look at the people down on the beach. You'll get the idea soon enough."

Suzi waited until he had pushed back the sliding screen, then raced into the kitchen, pouring out two cups of coffee from the percolator.

Then, as she had never purported to be a gourmet chef, she quickly toasted two iced strawberry Pop-Tarts, threw them on napkins and headed for the deck, their makeshift breakfast on a plastic tray she'd already equipped with containers of cream and sugar.

"How are you doing?" she asked, her back to him as she placed the tray on the glass-topped round table. Turning, she saw that he was standing at the far railing of the deck, alternately looking down at the beach and to the wide variety of beachfront condos lining the area as far to the north and south as he could see.

"I don't believe it," he said, his voice awestruck. "I don't bloody believe it! When I saw this place from the deck of the *Pegasus* it was nothing but sand and brush and birds. Have you Americans wrought a miracle, or cut a swath of destruction? Is this paradise—or hell?"

"Hell?" Suzi glanced to her right and left, then frowned. "I don't get it. You're looking at some of the choicest, highest priced real estate in Ocean City—and I've got the property tax receipt to prove it. Why would you think this is hell?"

He turned to her, grinning. "Well, not hell, precisely, and I suppose I shouldn't be surprised to see some development after one hundred and eighty-one years."

"Yes," Suzi said, noticing the way the sun lit small golden fires in his long hair, "we have managed to invent a thing or two."

"Of course. After all, my parents had never seen a gaslight, or water closets, in their youth. Each new generation does bring progressive thinking with it. But this place does smack of Sodom and Gomorrah, doesn't it, of a future run amuck? For instance, does everyone in America traipse around in public in their underclothes?"

Suzi shrugged. "Are you still complaining, Harry? Just think about it. You could have traveled *backward* through time and ended up in the seventeenth century. Which do you prefer—looking like a blond cover model, sure to be drooled over by all the voluptuous young women you see on the beach below us, or being surrounded by women dressed all in ugly gray wool from their toes to the tops of their heads, and then summarily being burned at the stake as some sort of warlock?"

"You have a point, madam, although I don't understand that term—cover model," Harry said, giving one last, rather interested look toward the beach and the half dozen bikini-clad young women playing volleyball on the sand. "Perhaps it is better in Ocean City after all. Would that by chance be my coffee?"

She followed him back to the table, deliberately seating herself in the shade of the umbrella stuck into the center of the glass top, because she was a natural blonde, and her skin tended to burn whenever she was even close to the sun.

"That's a pastry, sort of," she told him, pointing to the Pop-Tart. "Try it, you'll like it. But don't worry that you'll starve to death. I've already decided to phone my housekeeper in New York and have her come stay with us, because I don't think you're ready to eat at Jocelyn's—or any public place—at least not until you get used to being here."

Harry was already finished with his pastry and eyeing hers, so that she pushed it toward him. "Agreed," he said, taking a sip of coffee. "Do you think I'll be *here* for long?"

Suzi sat back against the orange-and-white director's chair and crossed her legs.

"Be here long? Cripes, Harry, how should I know? I don't know the faintest thing about time travel—because that's what you did, you know—travel through time. Unless I *have* gone bonkers, and a figment of my fertile imagination has just downed two strawberry Pop-Tarts in sixty seconds flat."

"I think it had something to do with the storm," Harry told her, ignoring her suggestion that he might not be real. "One of the sailors said I was to stay belowdecks, to keep out of the 'eye,' but I didn't listen to him."

"Yes, that's a failing of yours I already recognize," Suzi said, smiling.

He wagged his finger at her as if trying to put that finger on the solution to his journey from 1813. "That's it, of course. That strange storm. Everything has an explanation, if you only look for it. However, as I don't intend to brave any more storms from the deck of a ship, I suppose I am here to stay. There is no one in Sussex who will miss me, as I was an only child and my parents are deceased these last five years. I will just build myself a new life here in America. Yes, I believe I can live with that answer."

"I don't think you have a heck of a lot of choice, Harry, considering that you're stuck with having to make sense of the impossible or else lose your marbles. The real question is—can *I* learn to live with that answer?" Suzi teased, grinning openly now.

Really, Harry Wilde was a dear man. A little autocratic, but very dear. "However," she continued, "since we have no other choice but to work with the idea that you're here for keeps I'll have to get cracking. You can't live in that single outfit. And you don't even have shoes, just those thongs. I guess there's a silver lining to everything, Harry, because now I get to go shopping."

"Allow me to correct you, Suzi—please don't mind the informality, but you have, you know, been addressing me as Harry all morning long—*we* must go to the shops. I don't believe I care for your taste."

"You don't care for my—hey! The door's open downstairs, Harry, old sport. Feel free to leave at any the time. I'm sure you'll do just great out there on your own, with no money, and without the faintest idea how to behave."

He reached out and took her hand, sending a curious shiver up her arm—as if he didn't know that! "Now, Suzi, don't cut up stiff on me. I meant no harm."

She continued to glare at him, wishing he weren't so handsome when he smiled, wishing she wasn't such a gullible fool, wishing he was a nice, safe investment banker from the upper East Side with his own apartment and a Volvo whom she could take home to mother— if she still *had* a mother, which she didn't, so what did it matter, anyway?

But he *was* so very handsome, and she *was* a fool more accustomed to being tumbled around in the middle of an adventure than being boring and safe, and she was stuck here in her Ocean City condo with a romantic-looking, arrogant Regency hero in a muscle shirt.

Besides, hearing him say "Suzi" in his crisp English accent tickled her senses. Only slightly, of course. She wasn't the sort of female to go goo-goo over a man because of his accent. Was she?

No matter what, she might as well relax and go with the flow. After all, just like Harry, what other choice did she have?

"Look, Harry," she said, sighing. "Let's be reasonable about this, all right? You're not, as they say, really ready for prime-time playing yet, okay? So you just stay here—there's a television set in the living room you can watch while I'm gone—and I'll go buy you some more clothes. I'll even rustle up a couple of sandwiches—that's meat on bread—to hold you over until lunch."

"I would appreciate that very much, Miss Harper— Suzi. I feel as if I haven't eaten in a century, or perhaps two centuries."

"Very funny. Maybe you have a future as a comic. But don't worry. If you're lucky, Mrs. O'Reilly will be here before dinner tonight, so you won't starve. Between now and then, I'll take you on a tour of the condo, show you the light switches and all that stuff—don't ask, I'll explain later—and clue you in on a few things so you don't goof up and give yourself away. All right?"

Harry stood, and sliced another longing look toward the beach and, Suzi thought, bristling, the tanned, giggling, *bouncing* volleyball team. "Agreed, Suzi. Consider me your servant. Lead me to your television machine."

"You called me in Tokyo to ask me *what?* And at this hour of the night? Suzi, I've known and loved you for a long time, and I have tried with, I will admit, only varying levels of success, to understand how your mind works. I did my best to understand why you put a red rinse in your hair and served borscht at your dinner party after reading *The Hunt For Red October* as a way of showing appreciation for the book."

"I know, Courtney," Suzi said into the telephone she'd reluctantly had hooked up to service the day after Harry's appearance in her life, "and I'm grateful. But it wasn't just a dinner. It was my try at performance art, and you don't have to tell me how terrible it turned out. I had to wash my hair twice a day for a month to get rid of that rinse."

"Yes, well. That's only one example, Suzi. There's more. I didn't say anything when you took up skydiving because you thought it would be a good way to meet men who didn't still live with their mothers. And I refused to listen to Adam's rather biting remarks on the Op-ed piece you wanted to publish in the *Times* about favoritism toward the right-handed in today's society. But this tops Adam's list of 'the ten most unexplainable things Suzi's ever done!' And another thing—"

Suzi rolled her eyes at Harry and smiled at the receiver as she held it away from her ear. "Bad connection," she whispered, covering the mouthpiece, and Harry nodded, then pressed the remote control, once again on the lookout for the weathergirl on Channel Seven.

Suzi would be jealous, if she cared about Harry in "that" way, but as she didn't—well, she kept telling herself she didn't—she didn't mind that the weathergirl reminded him of someone he knew a long time ago. One hundred and eighty-one years ago, to be precise.

She placed the receiver against her ear once more to hear her good friend, Courtney Blackmun, bestselling novelist and wife of Adam Richardson, the senior senator from New Jersey, end with a sigh, "And why would you want to write a time-travel novel in the first place? You've always said the last, the very *last* thing you'd ever want to do is write a book. You said that it's far easier to be a reviewer and stand back launching grenades into the literary world than it would ever be to step onto the battlefield itself so someone like yourself could take potshots at you. That is what you said, isn't it?"

"Did I?" Suzi asked, pulling a face. "That sounds entirely too militaristic for me, Court. But listen. I apologize again for not thinking of the time difference, but I really do need help with this synopsis I'm writing. You did get my fax, didn't you? The one where I outlined my idea?"

"Yes, Suzi, I got it. But it's two a.m. here, and I'm exhausted. Can't I phone you in the morning? Adam has to meet with one of the Japanese foreign ministers, and I'll be free until four."

"Oh, sure," Suzi said, grimacing. "But by then it will probably be the middle of the night *here,* so that wouldn't work. Look, Courtney, old buddy, I said I'd never be so mean as to ever hold it over your head that I was the one who found Adam for you—"

"You loaned me your condo because I was suffering from writer's block, Suzi. *I* found Adam."

"Yeah, well, that's just semantics, isn't it? Like the way I took Sydney off your hands so you could be alone with Adam until you figured out he was right for you, even though *I* knew that the first moment I laid eyes on him. I did tell you how your dear daughter ran poor Mrs. O'Reilly bonkers with her practical tricks, didn't I? Not that I'm complaining, especially now that Syd's married and settling down, but you'd think, after all these years, that you might consider that you owed me one *teensy-weensy* little favor—"

"Break the connection, Suzi," Harry ordered imperiously, clicking off the television set. "Begging is beneath you, and most unbecoming in a lady of your age."

Suzi quickly covered the receiver and glared at Harry. Did he always have to harp on her age? Anyone would think she was old enough to be his mother!

"Will you please be quiet? This is women's business. It's how we operate. I'll have her wrapped around my little finger in three seconds flat. I—" She yanked the receiver back to her ear. "What did you say? Oh, Courtney, you're a doll! You want to know what? How long I've been working on this idea?"

She winced, looking to Harry, who was beginning to look more at home in her living room than Patchwork, who had shifted her loyalty to the newcomer and now slept at the foot of his bed. "Oh, about three weeks," she said, biting her bottom lip. "It's been going along pretty well so far, but now I've come to a sticky part."

"Trying to find a way to get identification for your time traveler," Courtney said. "Yes, I saw that in the fax. It's a tricky question. In fact, the whole notion of dealing with a man from another time is tricky."

"You don't know the *half* of it, Court," Suzi responded feelingly, looking toward her "tricky question," who was just then slipping on his sneakers, as if planning to go out on the beach without her—something she had expressly forbidden him to do. Not that her threats had stopped him yet.

The next time she went shopping she was going to buy him a leash! She covered the receiver yet again and barked, "Harry—*sit! Stay!*"

"Suzi? Do you have someone else there with you?" Courtney asked.

"Someone else with me?" Suzi parroted, smiling grimly as Harry winced at hearing her words and, for once, obeyed her. "No, Court. That's just the television. But I turned it off now. So, don't keep me in suspense. If you were writing this book, how would you handle the problem of identification?"

"I asked Adam," Courtney told her, and Suzi, hearing those magic words, immediately reached for a pen in order to take notes.

To Suzi's mind, asking Adam was almost on a par with anything to be found written on clay tablets—sensible, believable, and as safe as money in the bank. After all, not only was Adam a senator, but he was being touted as a vice-presidential nominee in the next election.

"Go on, Court," Suzi urged as Harry rose and came across the room to stand behind her, bending down to look over her shoulder at the still-blank piece of paper lying on the eighteenth-century English design mahogany desktop. "Tell me what he said. Tell me everything."

"Adam *said*," her friend informed her, "that for any alien—that includes your time traveler, Suzi—to gain identification without going through the normal immigration channels is illegal."

Suzi wrote it down: *illegal*.

"I can see now why he's such a trusted friend, Suzi," Harry sarcastically whispered into her free ear. "It takes a brilliant, top-rate mind to deduce that what we're asking to do is in violation of every legal precedent. I heard that term on CNN the other night," he added, smiling.

"Would you *please* put a lid on it," Suzi mouthed quietly, levering her free arm backward to give him a push. The man was a dedicated television junkie, and had learned more about her world in the past three weeks than she had cared to absorb in thirty-two years.

"However," Courtney went on, "as this is purely a fictional situation, as everyone knows time travel is nothing more than a romantic imagining..."

"Yeah, Court, pure fiction! You got that right," Suzi said brightly, once more turning her back on her resident fictional character.

"Yes, well," Courtney went on as Suzi began to feel *really* impatient with her friend, "seeing that it couldn't hurt to use such a device in fiction, Adam told me the best way for your hero to get bogus identification is through a criminal specializing in such things. There are probably a couple dozen people in that line of work in Manhattan alone, or so Adam told me. It's a problem he's trying to deal with in Washington."

"Really?" Suzi wrote: *problem*.

"Yes, indeed. The government is attempting to crack down on the practice at the federal level, and Congress wants to impose really stiff jail penalties for anyone who fakes an identification. Suzi? Are you still there? Did you hear me? Are you writing this down?"

"Sure, Court. Every word," Suzi promised, sitting stock-still, her pen frozen in her hand, her stomach suddenly relocating itself somewhere near her toes as she saw herself in prison stripes. "Every single word."

Chapter Four

Harry watched Suzi as she walked out of the ocean and pulled off her ridiculously flowered bathing cap, shaking her head so that her blond hair fell free and rearranged itself in a sleek curtain around her face.

A modern-day Venus rising from the sea, he thought, sighing, wondering if any artist, past or present, could do her justice.

Then his eyes fell to her figure, and the bright green bikini that had become the centerpiece of his daydreams these past two weeks or more, since she'd let him out of the house after their first, chaotic week of trying to get used to the idea that he had arrived in New Jersey direct from Regency England.

And it wasn't the house, but the *condo*, he corrected himself punctiliously, for he was always working, always concentrating on trying to become the complete gentleman of the late twentieth century.

Except when he was concentrating on Suzi's bikini, that was, and how she would look without it.

Thirty-two. The number was enough to boggle the mind. Ladies of two and thirty were supposed to be matrons, happily raising their children and bedeviling their husbands for gaming too deep, or on-the-shelf spinsters, definitely past their last prayers, and wearing silly white caps that tied beneath their chins.

Not that he'd say anything remotely like that to Suzanne Harper, who didn't seem to have the slightest notion that she was an old maid.

"Ah! That felt good! The water's always beautifully warm in August," Suzi declared, dropping to her knees on the blanket, dripping water everywhere.

"You are a creature of sensations, aren't you, Suzi? The texture of fudge against your teeth, the smell of the ocean, the feel of the waves breaking against your body. You're almost childlike sometimes," he commented, wiping stray droplets of water from the pages of the book he'd been trying, without much success, to read.

Watching Suzi jump the waves was far more interesting than history.

"So what? Don't patronize me, Harry. Really, you ought to try it, instead of roasting here on the blanket, reading Professor Blakeheart's book. No matter how you slice it, the war ended in a draw. Although I still think it stinks that you guys burnt down our capital."

"Why? From what I've seen on the news programs, your own citizens are doing a pretty good job of destroying the entire city, one block at a time. Aren't you chilled?''

He looked at her as she unashamedly knelt in front of him; her hair delightfully mussed, her small nose sun-kissed, small rivulets of water lazily running down her body, along her feminine curves, sliding beneath the slick green fabric just at the enticing curve of her breasts.

A single droplet leisurely made its way lower, toward her navel, coming to rest in that delightful indentation.

He really wished she wouldn't sit so close. She was beginning to interfere with his breathing.

"Cold? No, not really. Oh, I get it. You want me to cover up, don't you? You're such a gentleman, Harry, if a bit stuffy sometimes." Suzi obligingly slipped her head and arms into the green-and-white striped caftan and wriggled its length down over her hips before sitting back on the blanket. "There. Better now?"

Harry swallowed once, trying to bring some moisture into his suddenly dry mouth. "Much. I know I've attempted to conform to your American mores, and I agree that you are wearing nothing out of the ordinary, but for the life of me I can't seem to become accustomed to this practice of parading about half naked. My friends and I used to watch ladies descending from their carriages, praying for a glimpse of ankle."

As he said the words his mind conjured up a mental picture of Suzi as she would appear in Regency dress. Her small, slim body fashionably clothed in dainty sprigged muslin, a large straw hat fetchingly tied beneath her chin, a silly parasol shading her little nose from the sun as she sat up beside him and they tooled his horses through the park for the promenade.

He swallowed again, the thought doing more to excite him, and his imagination, than the reality of Suzi in her bright green bikini.

How strange. How exceedingly strange.

"You know, Harry," Suzi said, interrupting his uncomfortable thoughts just as he was imagining what it would be like to shock the *ton* by kissing Miss Suzanne Harper in the middle of Hyde Park, "we'll soon have to go back to Manhattan. I'd only planned to stay at the condo until the end of August, and although I could do my reviews from here, I've got a few social engagements for September that I simply can't get out of. Especially Wilbur's dinner party. Nobody misses one of those."

"Wilbur," Harry repeated, nodding. "That would be Wilbur Langley, head of Langley Publishing. He's the one you said might be able to help us get identification after you all but hung up on your friend Courtney the other night without listening to what she had to say. How would a publisher know about such things?"

Suzi rolled her huge, beguiling eyes. "Wilbur, dear Harry, knows something about *everything*. That's a large part of his charm. I don't know why I didn't go to him in the first place. Wilbur's a real Renaissance man, with a lovely touch of Phineas T. Barnum thrown in. Phineas T. was a showman—you know, a circus master?"

"He puts on horse shows, like at Astley's in London?" Harry was confused, not an unusual circumstance these past three weeks and two days, but one he was becoming used to. "I don't understand."

Suzi ran a hand through her hair, a habit she had whenever she was thinking deeply. "Wrong analogy. Sorry about that. I keep forgetting that your English and American English are sometimes two different languages. No, he doesn't show horses."

"You'll have to explain."

"I'm trying, Harry. Wilbur is—well, Wilbur is just Wilbur. He's crowding seventy now, although you'd never believe it to look at him. He's got more money than almost anyone I know and only dabbles in the publishing business anymore, allowing his ex-son-in-law, Daniel Quinn, to take care of everything. You'll love Daniel and his wife, Joey. She was once his chauffeur—his coachman—but now she's a bestselling author. They have four of the most wonderful children..."

She raised a hand to wave off his questions. "Never mind. It would be impossible to explain. Besides, I'm getting off the point. Wilbur is a patron of the arts, knowledgeable in politics and finance, and a lover of fine foods, although he's also got a puckish love of mischief in his soul. He dresses like something straight out of GQ, that's a man's fashion magazine, and still has women falling all over him."

Suzi sighed. "I guess you could say he's a Regency gentleman. Yes! That's it! Wilbur's a cross between Beau Brummell, Lord Byron and your Prince Regent."

"He's sounds extremely interesting, if a bit intimidating." Harry stood and shook out the blanket, as Suzi gathered up her belongings in preparation for a return to the condo. "When can I meet him?"

"Meet him? You've been out in the sun too long." Suzi laughed out loud, a lovely, trilling laugh that Harry had already learned he enjoyed hearing. "Good Lord, Harry, I'd never let you *meet* him!"

They trekked back through the hot sand, heading for the condo. "Now I am confused," Harry admitted, opening the door and taking hold of Suzi's arm, keeping her from heading straight for the shower. "Why can't I meet the man? Are you afraid I'll give myself away? I didn't raise anyone's suspicions last night, when you took me to that strange restaurant."

"Oh, yeah. Right. You asked for a finger bowl, Harry, for crying out loud. At a place with golden arches outside. Harry, at a fast-food restaurant that doesn't even include *plates* with the meal, didn't you think you might have been pushing things just a little?"

"All right. So I made one simple mistake," he conceded, remembering the look on the attendant's face when he'd asked for the finger bowl after being forced to eat his french fries with his hands.

And he would admit he was still having some difficulty resigning himself to the idea that people would wish to wipe their mouths with paper rather than finely pressed linen, too, but he wouldn't bore Suzi with that complaint again.

"But," he persisted, "this Langley fellow sounds like a fine sort, a man of the world. We'd probably rub along together extremely well."

"Uh-uh. No. Not in this lifetime. Trust me in this, Harry. We don't want Wilbur within ten miles of you. I'll just use the same story on him that I used on Courtney. And you have to admit it was a brilliant idea. Good old Court fell for it without a hitch, and I see no reason for Wilbur to sniff out a problem."

"Really, my dear? And I had so thought you believed me to be penetratingly astute. How sad."

Both Harry and Suzi whirled to face the still-open door.

"Wilbur!" Suzi exclaimed, quickly shaking her arm free of Harry's grip. "Darling! How good to see you." Her eyes narrowed speculatively as she took a single step toward the man standing in the doorway, then stopped. "Er, exactly *why* am I seeing you, Wilbur?"

Harry stood by silently, taking his measure of the tallish man who, with a wave of one manicured hand and a slight bow of his silvery head, wordlessly asked permission to enter the foyer of the condo, then allowed Suzi to kiss his cheek.

Now here was a man who knew how to outfit himself, Harry decided, instantly impressed with the publisher's light gray, double-breasted suit, the startlingly white, highly starched shirt with collar edges as sharp as knifepoints, the mauve silk neck cloth—his *necktie,* he mentally corrected—exquisitely arranged and neatly accented by a small diamond stickpin.

"You're seeing me, dear Suzi, because our mutual friend and your self-appointed guardian, Courtney, telephoned me from Tokyo begging me to come to this backwater because *our* mutual friend—that would be you, Suzi—is once more showing signs of having perhaps taken an unfortunate, brain-scrambling blow to the head. From what I overheard as I arrived, I'd say Courtney has once more proven herself to be the next best thing to a soothsayer. Was it a topple down those ridiculous spiral stairs that did the damage this time?''

Sensing Suzi's panic, and not the sort to comfortably fade into the background, Harry stepped forward, his right hand outstretched, a bright smile on his face, and said bracingly, ''Mr. Langley, how very good to meet you. Allow me to introduce myself. The name is Wilde. Harry Wilde, on holiday from Britain. Please excuse my ramshackle attire. Won't you please come upstairs to the sitting room? Mrs. O'Reilly, Suzanne's housekeeper, is not in at the moment, having discovered a kindred spirit in Suzanne's neighbor, Mrs. O'Connell, so that she spends the majority of her time with the lady. But I am convinced Suzanne is up to brewing us a pot of tea. Suzanne?''

''Hmm?'' Suzi questioned distractedly, looking to him with naked appeal in her large blue eyes. ''I missed something. What did you say, Harry?''

''He said,'' Wilbur intervened smoothly, winking at Harry, ''that you should run along now to have your shower and put on your prettiest dress so that we might allow my chauffeur to drive us to Atlantic City for dinner. You're rather sandy, in case you haven't noticed, and smell of the sea. Harry will join me upstairs, where we men will somehow manage to make our own tea sans Mrs. O'Reilly's assistance. Take your time, my dear. I am convinced Harry and I will be able to entertain ourselves in your absence. He can bathe and dress later, while you and I catch up on all the New York gossip you've missed."

"Oh, no," Suzi protested, grabbing Harry's arm as if afraid he was going to immediately announce that he was a traveler who was visiting from Britain, all right—from nineteenth-century Britain. "That can't be what Harry said, Wilbur. I mean—"

"Suzanne." Harry bit out the word through clenched teeth, his tone heavy with meaning, which he knew might frighten her, but then there were times when a gentleman had to assert himself. "Please go do as Mr. Langley says. We'll be just fine."

Harry felt sorry for Suzi, he really did, but he had a strong urge to be alone with Mr. Wilbur Langley for a few minutes, to engage the man in conversation—if only to test himself on what he believed to be his rather excellent acclimatization to the twentieth-century world.

Besides, if he could learn the name of the man's tailor it would go a long way toward reconciling himself to his temporary, and totally unsuitable Ocean City wardrobe. At the moment, he was feeling decidedly underdressed in his bathing trunks and the same muscle shirt Suzi had presented him with that eventful morning three short weeks ago.

"Oh, all right," Suzi declared at last, looking as if she was about to burst into tears. "But don't you dare say anything—" she sneaked a quick look at Wilbur, then blurted, rather helplessly, Harry thought "—anything about *us.*"

"Ah! Do I sense a blossoming romance?" Wilbur inquired, waving a blushing Suzi on her way and motioning for Harry to precede him up the spiral staircase. "How very intriguing, to say the least. I never pictured Suzi with an Englishman. A fortune-hunting race car driver or globe-trotting polo player perhaps, although I suppose that wouldn't preclude the man's being English."

Harry bit on his bottom lip, knowing he should say nothing about the glaringly obvious fact that, at thirty-two, Suzi was more than a little long in the tooth to interest him, and led the way up to the sitting room. No. The *living* room. Had he already slipped, and referred to it as the sitting room? That would be too bad. Really, he must monitor his tongue every moment if he and Suzi were to carry this off!

"As it's already gone five, I don't believe I should mind a glass of sherry as a substitute for tea," Wilbur said as he settled himself into a chair as if very much at home in the condo. "Suzi keeps some for me, as I recall, for I am always finding myself summoned to this place, tending to various crises in the lives of all my favorite people. Courtney and her Adam, her darling daughter, Sydney, this past year, and of course to visit with Daniel and Joey and my grandchildren. I must consider purchasing my own domicile on the beach. It is rather relaxing here, isn't it, in its own small way?"

Harry sought out the sherry and three glasses, smiling noncommittally as he took up a chair across from Wilbur's. "So, Mr. Langley," he said after a long moment during which he could feel the older man inspecting him, "you've heard from Miss Blackmun? Was it something to do with Suzi's desire to write a novel?"

"Ah, you know about that, do you? It would prove extremely interesting—a novel written by our dearest Suzi. Although I don't believe I'll ever see the completed manuscript." Wilbur's vivid blue eyes narrowed as if measuring him in some way. "That would place you in this condo for some time, wouldn't it? Did you meet on the beach? A romantic place, the Ocean City beach, if my past experience with beautiful New York women transported to its smooth sands is any indication."

Harry looked into his glass, deliberately avoiding Wilbur's all-too-intelligent eyes. "Yes, as a matter of fact, Mr. Langley, we did meet on the beach. Just at dawn. It was highly romantic, actually."

"Yes, Suzi is very into romantic situations. Also bizarre situations, as I know to my sorrow. She can't help it. Things just seem to *happen* to Suzi. Strange things that would never happen to anyone else." He paused for a moment, definitely, Harry decided, for effect, then asked, "Are you a strange thing, Harry?"

Suzi had been right this time, Harry decided, hiding a grimace. He shouldn't have come within ten miles of Wilbur Langley. "Strange, Mr. Langley?" he repeated, trying to chuckle. "In what way?"

Wilbur smiled. "Time will tell, won't it, Harry? And, please, call me Wilbur. Everyone does."

"All right. Wilbur." Harry knew the man was trying to put him at his ease, and he fought the sensation to allow him to succeed. "You mentioned Atlantic

City earlier, Wilbur. I believe Suzi mentioned something about games of chance in that city. Do you gamble?''

"I'm in publishing, Harry. That, in my humble opinion, is always a gamble. To take someone's idea, someone's vision of reality, and turn it into a successful piece of fiction—I do adore fiction, you understand—is always a gamble. Do you read, Harry?''

Harry closed his eyes for a moment, doing his best to recall the name of a contemporary author he'd seen on a television talk show the day before. It wouldn't do him much good to name Shakespeare, or Milton, or Sheridan, as his favorites, and it might do him great harm.

"Grisham," he said at last, smiling as his mind captured the name. "John Grisham. He's quite interesting, don't you think? And extremely successful."

"Immensely," Wilbur answered, taking another sip of sherry. "Although my taste runs more to romantic fiction than legal thrillers. Are you, perhaps, like Mr. Grisham, a lawyer?''

Very neat, Wilbur, Harry thought. You pry, but you pry discreetly. "No," he answered, smiling. "For my sins, I, too, am a writer. Although I have not as yet seen any of my work published."

"A writer? A novelist, perhaps? Perhaps I have stumbled on something. Perhaps you are a novelist attempting to write a novel on *time travel?* That would make more sense than trying to believe that Suzi has decided to dabble in science fiction."

Harry felt his hackles beginning to rise. "I am not attempting to use Suzi in order to establish a career,

Wilbur. I am not without my own resources." He said this last without flinching, although he knew whatever "resources" held in his name in his London banks and on the Exchange had long since gone either to his third-cousin heirs or the Crown.

"Dear boy, whatever makes you think I am suggesting anything of the kind? It can only be a coincidence that you have taken up residence here with Suzi—and you have taken up residence here, haven't you? It can only be a coincidence that you are a writer and Suzi is a well-known, respected reviewer with ties to many of the most prestigious publishing houses in Manhattan. No more than serendipity, I'm sure."

"Here I am!" Suzi announced breathlessly as she all but stumbled from the spiral staircase, her hair damp from her shower, and still working to close the topmost buttons of the dress she had worn the first day she and Harry had met. "You can take your shower, Harry," she said, glaring at him meaningfully. *"Now."*

Harry, grateful for her timely, if heavy-handed rescue, quickly excused himself and headed downstairs, brushing past Suzi as he went, but unable to look her in the eye.

But don't you dare say anything—anything about us.

She may only have been trying to warn him to keep his mouth shut, but on a scale of one to ten, it still had to be about the *stupidest* thing Suzi believed she had ever said. And to say it within earshot of Wilbur Langley? Well, that took the statement out of the realm of stupid and pushed it straight up to completely idiotic!

Throughout the drive into Atlantic City and most of dinner, Wilbur had been looking at her oddly. It was almost as if he was torn between wanting to congratulate her for finally falling in love with a man who appeared somewhat normal—ha! if Wilbur only knew!—and wondering if she was in some sort of trouble.

How could she be in trouble? Just because she was harboring an alien, planning to procure him illegal identification and then still be at a total loss as to what to *do* with the man once he was no longer in danger of being deported?

Why would anyone consider that trouble?

And if she had begun to look at Harry Wilde in an altogether other light, one that had a lot more to do with her personal feelings for him than her worries over his problems, well, what of it? It wasn't as if Harry were falling in love with her. He couldn't be.

According to the rules of society in Harry's time, she was older than the flood, and good for nothing more than sitting in a corner with an ugly purple turban on her head, knitting slippers, or whatever it was old maids did in Regency England.

In Harry's Regency-era mind, an eighteen-year-old bride was his desired mate, which was just about the silliest thing Suzi could imagine. What eighteen-year-old could possibly pull off marriage to a man who still didn't ''get'' the distinction between the rock star Prince and the Prince of Wales?

And why did Wilbur have to show up, anyway? Wasn't it just like Courtney to smell a rat in that phone call she'd made to Japan, and then send Wilbur running hotfoot to investigate? What did they think she was? Helpless? Accident prone? Capable of getting herself into trouble at the drop of a hat?

Okay. So maybe she didn't have such a great track record. Maybe she did tend to bite off more than she could comfortably chew once in a while. Maybe she did seem to have a penchant for trouble, for odd situations, for jumping into water that was over her head.

She had been on her own since her early twenties, when her wealthy parents and only uncle had died in a plane crash, but she hadn't frittered away her considerable inheritance or married the first ski bum she'd met.

She had finished college, graduating with honors, no less, and gotten work at *Literary Lines,* a damn respectable book review magazine, and if she only freelanced now, taking more time for herself now that the remainder of her trust fund had been turned over to her at the age of thirty, she still hadn't done anything ridiculous.

She was simply a free spirit, a woman who liked her independance and enjoyed trying new things.

Like bungee jumping from a West Virginia bridge.

Like meditation, in India.

Like tofu hamburgers at her dinner party to which Senator Adam Richardson had brought an unexpected guest—the president's nominee for attorney general.

What was so wrong with any of that?

"Suzi?"

She shook herself mentally and brought her mind back to attention, having slipped away into her own world halfway through the main course at the casino restaurant.

What in the world was the matter with her? She couldn't afford to lose her concentration for an instant when Wilbur and Harry were talking. At any minute Harry could make some mortal slip, like telling Wilbur about his near speed-record-breaking monthlong ocean crossing from Portsmouth. "Yes? What did you say, Wilbur? I'm afraid I was wool-gathering."

"That's quite all right, my dear. Young love does have a way of muddling the brain," Wilbur said, smiling at her so that she longed to kick Harry under the table. Why hadn't he disabused Wilbur of the idea that the two of them were lovers? A better question— why hadn't she?

"Wilbur suggested we visit the casino, Suzi," Harry said, his eyes positively glowing with interest. Damn the man. Was there ever a Regency dandy who didn't like to gamble? Whose money did he think he'd be spending? He certainly couldn't pull out one of the pile of gold pieces he'd had stuffed in his pouch!

"How lovely," Suzi said, her smile more of a grimace as she looked at Harry, dressed in the navy blue sports jacket she had bought him, his blond hair tied back at his nape.

He did look wonderful, even with his long hair. He looked wonderful, intriguing, sexy, and if he didn't stop smiling at her she was going to pick up her butter knife and stab him! "I suppose I wouldn't mind losing a few quarters in the slot machines."

"Slot machines. Ah, yes, I understand. Slot machines are a female's quaint notion of gambling, Harry," Wilbur said informatively, his smile taking any sting out of his words. "Actually, Suzi, Harry and I are going to try our hands at the baccarat table."

"Baccarat?" Suzi felt her heart taking the express elevator to her toes. "Was that inven—that is, does Harry know how to play?"

"I've explained the rules," Wilbur told her, "and Harry is extremely interested."

"I'll just bet he is," Suzi muttered under her breath.

"Shall we get you a few rolls of quarters and let you play while we men investigate our options?" asked Wilbur. "Harry has volunteered an interest in the blackjack tables as well, you understand, so we might be a while."

"Oh, goody," Suzi said, her smile painful.

"Now, now, Suzi. Don't pout," Wilbur scolded genially. "You two talk it over while I go settle the bill, all right? I'll meet you at the main entrance to the casino floor."

Suzi's smile stayed glued in place until Wilbur had placed his arm around the young waitress's slim waist and guided her toward the cash register, before turning quickly to Harry, her eyes narrowed dangerously. "Harry Wilde! Are you out of your *tiny mind?*"

He patted her hand comfortingly, an action that made her want to scream at him. "Now, Suzi, don't go flying into the treetops. Wilbur and I are rubbing along together quite famously. And I'm not about to stumble now and do anything revealing."

"If I were a betting woman—which I am *not*— I wouldn't put a bent nickel on your odds of keeping Wilbur from becoming suspicious."

"You're in danger of becoming overset, Suzi, and for no reason. I didn't say anything when I saw that vehicle he called a limousine, did I? It's nothing like your car, and it even has a television machine. You Americans can't do anything without a television machine close to hand, can you? Not that I'm complaining. If it weren't for all the news programs I've been watching I wouldn't have known how to answer when Wilbur questioned me about our new prime minister. He has quite an impressive smile, doesn't he? Do you suppose he uses that toothpaste that makes teeth whiter and brighter?"

Suzi placed her elbow on the table and sighed, resting her forehead against her hand. The man was a walking commercial, and a fountain of misinformation ever since he'd discovered the daily soap operas. To Harry, all the world was filled with political tyrants, partisan politics, commercials for everything from hemorrhoidal creams to personal computers and now, the sexual adventures of daytime television.

"Harry," she said—pleaded—looking up at him through her lashes. "I don't know how much more of this I can take. Honestly. No, you didn't go all bug-eyed when you saw Wilbur's limousine. However, he might have suspected a little something out of the ordinary when you first saw the lights of the casinos and wondered aloud how many *gas lamps* it took to make such a glow."

He waved his hands in front of his face, pushing away her objections. "I'm on familiar territory now, Suzi. There wasn't a gaming house in London I didn't visit, and I am, I must say with all modesty, fairly good with the cards. I'll just watch Wilbur for a while, and take my cues from him. You have nothing to worry about. Honestly you don't. I promise that I won't let the game out of the bag. And I'll repay you from my winnings—with interest."

He accepted the money she handed him, then stood behind her and held out her chair. "That's let the *cat* out of the bag, or give the game *away,* Harry. Just stick to your own language, okay? American English is still beyond you. And you're right. Your modesty overwhelms me. Oh, and stop being so nice to me. Wilbur's ready to send out invitations to the wedding."

She froze, turning hot and cold by turns, as Harry bent forward and placed a lingering kiss on her nape. "Harry!" she exclaimed, startled, looking into his smiling face. "We're in public, for crying out loud, where anybody could see you. Why did you do that?"

He took her hand and led her through the maze of tables and toward the casino. "You walk around in *public* half naked and ask me why I believed it permissible to kiss you in a darkened restaurant? You Americans kiss all the time, and even go to bed in public."

"That's not what I meant and you know it. And we don't go to bed in public. How many times must I tell you that those are actors in a soap opera."

"Then you're really asking why I kissed you," he said pleasantly, waving to Wilbur, who was waiting for them, already holding several rolls of quarters. Obviously he intended to get Harry to himself for a while, shunting her off to the slot machines.

"All right," Suzi answered grudgingly, shrugging her shoulders. She really didn't want to discuss the subject anymore, but she was still interested in his answer. "Why did you kiss me?

She nearly tripped on the smooth rug when Harry answered calmly, "I kissed you, dear Miss Suzanne Harper, because I'm slowly beginning to understand the attraction American men have with older women. Something about them becoming not older, but somehow *better*."

Chapter Five

Suzi stood at the edge of the driveway, a wide smile pasted on her face as she and Harry stood arm in arm and waved goodbye to Wilbur.

Then, as the limousine's softly glowing taillights disappeared down the street and into the night, she took off Harry's arm, whirled around on her heels and stomped back to the condo.

Harry raced after her, not convinced she wouldn't slam the door in his face, leaving him to sleep on the beach. He slipped into the foyer just as she was pushing on the door and took hold of her arm.

"Oh, no, you don't," he warned, pulling her toward the staircase. "You're not going to look daggers at me all the way back from Atlantic City and then disappear into your bedchamber without an explanation."

"That's bedroom, Harry—not bedchamber," she bit out angrily, then shrugged. "Oh, very well. You want to hear why I'm upset? You really want to hear it? Okay, buster, I'll tell you. *Boy,* will I tell you!"

Giving him a none-too-gentle shove in the center of his chest, she pushed past him and made her way upstairs and into the living room, where she nearly threw herself onto the couch.

She was like a child giving into a tantrum, and she was infinitely appealing.

He followed after her, more than a little amused by her outburst of temper, and took up a chair across the room, motioning with his hand that she was now free to lambaste him with her complaints.

"You won over six thousand dollars, you idiot!" she exclaimed, obviously beginning with her most important complaint, sitting forward as if she had been turned into a spitting cat ready to spring.

Was that all? He grinned, still rather pleased with himself. Using today's exchange rate on the financial news, how would that translate into pounds, he wondered idly, his grin fading as Suzi went on the attack once more.

"Don't look so damned pleased with yourself, Harry Wilde! Do you know what would have happened if Wilbur hadn't stepped in and said that he'd won that money and you were only helping him carry the chips?"

"No, Suzi, I don't. But I am confident that you will not allow that lack of knowledge to continue."

"Oh, don't be so bloody British! And you're darn right I won't! The IRS would have asked you for your social security number, so that you could pay taxes on your winnings—that's what would have happened. Only you don't *have* a social security number, do you, Mr. Harry Wilde? So now not only does Wilbur have to pay taxes on *your* winnings, but he smells a rat—he smells a *big* rat.''

She beat her closed fists on the cushions on either side of her. ''Lord, I could cheerfully murder Courtney for calling him and asking him to check up on me! Why does everybody think they have to help me? Do they think I'm incapable of doing anything myself? And don't you dare to answer that question, Harry. Not if you want to sleep here tonight!''

Harry frowned, trying to concentrate on Suzi's main argument. ''The IRS?'' He shook his index finger, trying to remember where he'd heard those letters before. ''Oh, yes. That would be the Internal Revenue Service. Your government's collecting arm for taxes, isn't that correct?'' He frowned. ''How much revenue will they require from Wilbur? I'll have to reimburse him, of course.''

Suzi rolled her eyes, still looking as if she wanted to punch something. Or somebody. He was glad he had chosen to sit across the room. ''Sure you do. And exactly how do you plan to do that, Harry? Send him a check? You don't have any checks, Harry. You don't have a bank account. And do you know why? I'll tell you why. *Because you don't exist!*''

She fell back against the cushions, folding her arms across her stomach. ''Of course, that's the least of our problems. Wilbur's on to us now, Harry. You can count on that. He knows you're illegal—boy, are you illegal! He may have said he bought my story that it would be easier for him to claim all the winnings as his because he's an American citizen and you're a British subject, but he was only playing along."

"Playing along?"

"Yes, pretending to believe that there's nothing the least bit strange about you. Count on it, Harry. Wilbur might be gone, but he'll be back. He's probably on his car phone to Scotland Yard right now, checking to make sure you aren't some escaped ax murderer I decided to bring home to dinner."

"You are overreacting," Harry declared, bravely going over to sit beside her on the couch, and fighting the niggling feeling that she might be right.

"Really? Okay, wise guy, convince me." Suzi dared, glaring at him.

"Wilbur doesn't believe you to be that poor a judge of character, for one thing. Otherwise, he would never have gone back to Manhattan tonight."

"Who says he's gone?" Suzi countered. "I'll bet you the tax we owe the man that he's off the phone with Scotland Yard and is checking himself into that new luxury hotel down the street even as we speak. Oh, Harry," she wailed, laying her head against his shoulder, "we're in for it now."

The possibility that they might be in trouble disconcerted Harry, but not nearly as much as Suzi's presence excited him. Slipping his arm up and around her shoulders, he used his free hand to pat her bare arm, promising, "I won't allow Wilbur's suspicions to upset you, Suzi. I'll leave immediately."

Her head shot up and she stared at him, her wide blue eyes shocked as she pressed a hand against his chest. "Leave? But you can't leave. Where would you go? The local New Jersey retirement home for nineteenth-century time travelers? Harry—don't be ridiculous!"

This was nice. She didn't want him to leave. She also was sitting very intimately pressed against him. That was also nice. Very nice. Almost inspiring.

"You want me to stay, Suzi?" he asked, lifting one side of his mouth in a smile he'd been told by one forward young Mayfair miss was "rather unnerving, Harry, truly."

"Don't go reading anything into this, Harry," Suzi warned, although she didn't pull away from him. "I'm kind to dumb animals, too."

"Really? You must tell me about these ignorant animals. Do you also pay their gambling debts?"

Now she did move away, only far enough so that she could give him a playful swat. "No, silly. I give them something to eat and send them on their way. The way I should have done with you."

"Feed them? Now that you mention it, I *am* a little hungry." He leaned forward and began nibbling on her ear. "Um, that tastes good."

"Harry! Stop that!" Suzi protested, although he was quick to notice that she didn't pull away but, rather, only tilted her head slightly so that he could gain even closer access to her throat, the sweet smell of her hair, the tantalizing texture of her skin. "Really, Harry," she whispered huskily, "you must stop that."

Harry was feeling nothing if not amenable. He'd stop nuzzling her neck. Gladly. Because if he stopped nuzzling her neck he would be free to kiss her lips.

Her soft, pouting, cherry red lips.

Did they taste of cherries as well? Or would they taste of heaven, of delights that would take him above the problems of the earth?

He decided to find out.

Pressing Suzi back against the cushions of the couch, he levered himself forward, then turned to face her, placing a finger beneath her chin.

"Harry?" Suzi fairly squeaked. "You don't want to do this. I—I'm too old for you, for one thing—"

Harry concentrated his vaguely amused, definitely appreciative gaze on Suzi's slightly open mouth. "I've been thinking about that. Allowing for my trip through time, dear heart, I'm two hundred and sixteen. You couldn't possibly be too old for me."

He watched, entranced, as the corners of her mouth lifted in amusement. "You have a point, Harry," she said softly, and he felt her hand cupping the back of his neck. "Maybe I'm too *young* for you?"

He lowered his head another fraction. "I don't think so, Suzi. But you do talk too much," he chastened gently before closing the gap and touching his mouth to hers.

Harry didn't know if his reaction was so strong and immediate because he had been without a woman for the two months he had been at sea, or if it was because he had been without a woman for one hundred and eighty-one years, or if it was because Suzi Harper was the woman he was kissing.

He didn't, couldn't, know what was making him feel as he did now, as if he could kiss this woman until the world came crashing down around him and never be sorry.

He only knew that Suzi Harper was in his arms, her mouth sweetly open beneath his, her body curved intimately against his, her spread hands pressing against his back, her acceptance of his kiss at once startling and somehow natural, as if this moment was meant to be. Had always been meant to be.

Br-r-ring! Br-r-ring!

"Ignore it," he grumbled against her lips as she stiffened in his arms. Harry appreciated the immediacy of modern communication such as the telephone, which was certainly an improvement over the pennypost, but there were times when there was a lot to be said for the slower pace of what Suzi insisted upon terming Regency England.

She pushed her hands against his forearms. "I can't, Harry. It's Wilbur."

He collapsed against the couch cushions, his breathing disturbingly ragged, as she struggled to her feet, stepping over his legs as she made her way to the telephone. He couldn't seem to recover from their kiss as rapidly as she, and prudently remained on the couch.

"How above all things wonderful!" he managed to say. "Not only is she beautiful, but the woman's clairvoyant as well."

The phone rang again, insistently.

"Put a sock in it, Harry," Suzi ordered, smoothing down the skirt of her dress as she lifted her chin, ready to do battle. "I'm not clairvoyant. It just figures that it's Wilbur, checking up on me."

Silently agreeing that Mrs. O'Reilly, who had temporarily moved in with Mrs. O'Connell in order to lend the old woman some company during a flare-up of her arthritis, left much to be desired in the way of a chaperone, Harry nodded, agreeing with Suzi's conclusion.

"Hello!" Suzi said, rather breathlessly, Harry noticed with a smile as she pointedly turned her back on his amusement. So, she wasn't so unaffected after all. That was nice.

He listened during Suzi's silence, as if he could somehow hear the conversation taking place at the other end of the telephone.

"Wilbur, that's so sweet of you!" Suzi exclaimed at last. "You've what?" She turned toward Harry once more, shaking her head. "They don't just rent? They actually *sell* the apartments? How, um, how perfectly *wonderful* that you should be considering the idea!" Her grimace was comical. "Yes, I do know the place. It's a lovely building ... and the units are completely furnished?"

She shook her fist at Harry as he began to laugh, any thoughts of romance now effectively fled with Wilbur's telephone call. "What?" Suzie was saying. "Breakfast? *Tomorrow?* Just you and me? You want to discuss Harry's problem? What problem. Harry doesn't have any problems. Oh. Oh, I see. All right. If you want to be nasty about it, yes, Harry does need some identification. Well, I don't—"

Harry fell head down lengthwise on the couch, prudently stuffing his face into one of the pillows as his laughter escaped him. Watching Suzi try to side-step Wilbur Langley's obvious insistence that they meet tomorrow morning was better than having a box seat for the farce at Covent Garden.

He felt a slap on his back.

"You can come up for air now, Harry," Suzi told him as he turned onto his back and looked up over the edge of the throw pillow and into her clearly angry features. "Wilbur's going to tell us how to get you identification. He says," she hesitated a moment, then went on, "Wilbur says we can do it ourselves, without involving anyone else. He says—"

Harry jackknifed to his feet, staring at Suzi across the coffee table. "How does he know I've traveled through time?"

"He doesn't," Suzi said, turning for the stairs. "He simply thinks you're here illegally and has given you the benefit of the doubt that there is a good reason behind what you've done—sneaking into the country. He *likes* you, if you can believe that, and thinks you're a good, honest man at heart."

"And since I'm so good and honest, *he's* decided he's willing to break the law for me?" Harry asked, hurriedly following after Suzi as she made her way down the spiral staircase.

Something about Wilbur's reasoning didn't ring true, but for the moment Harry was far more concerned for Suzi. "He'd allow *you* to break the law? A man who is so obviously protective of you. Why?"

Suzi stood just inside her bedroom, her face small and pinched, her eyes like saucers. "Because my old friend Wilbur's a firm believer in the course of true love running smooth, or words to that effect," she answered dully. "Personally I think he's finally going senile. Love has nothing to do with why I want you to get identification. Absolutely *nothing!*"

Before Harry could play the cad and remind her that she had appeared to be a willing, if not yet loving, participant in the lovemaking that had barely begun before Wilbur's call had so importunely interrupted, the door slammed in his face and he heard the lock turn.

Smiling in pleasant bemusement, and reflectively scratching his head, Harry retired to his own bed-chamber—*bedroom*— feeling pretty much in charity with the entire wild and wonderful world he had been transported to three short weeks ago.

It was hot, even for New Jersey at the end of August, and Suzi wished she had thought to bring an insulated container of ice tea with her. A jug, and perhaps a map. Most certainly a flyswatter. The place was simply crawling with mosquitoes and other bugs she preferred not to give a name to.

This was the third cemetery they'd checked, she and Harry, and it looked as if they would soon have to pile back into her car and find a fourth. And all because Harry was being such a royal pain in the neck!

"I still don't believe I'm doing this!" she exclaimed, stopping beneath the shade of a tree and turning to glare at her stubborn time traveler. "We found one in the first cemetery, and two in the second. What's your problem anyway, Harry? *Why* can't you be satisfied?''

She watched as he bent to look at another headstone, his skin bronzed from the sun, the nearly white dusting of hair on his arms and legs almost giving his body a golden glow.

For a guy who had claimed not to like modern dress, he was doing a great impersonation of a golden beach boy in his shorts and muscle shirt. And if he ever cut his hair, that glorious, sun-streaked blond hair, she just might strangle him.

But she didn't, as Wilbur had supposed, love the man. At times like these, when he proved to be so infuriatingly pigheaded, she wasn't even entirely convinced she particularly *liked* him.

"The name has to be exactly right," he said as he stood once more, shaking his head. "Not just the year of birth, but the name. I refuse to spend the remainder of my life as an Ignatius or a Frank."

"Or a Johann," Suzi said, stepping back out into the sun in order to follow him down the next row. "I know, I know. You want a good, solid, English name. Like *Harry,* as if it was the be-all and end-all of great names. Personally, old sport, I'm not all that cracked up over it.''

He was bending down once more, balancing himself on his haunches. "If I'm going to have to take on a new identity, I have to feel comfortable with it. It's not enough that the person was born in 1959. Now, here's one that might suit.''

She dropped to her knees beside him and leaned forward to peer at the small heart-shaped stone. It wasn't easy, for the remote graveyard was rather old and run-down, the grass even in this relatively newer section grown up around the stones as if no one cared about this place, about what it meant.

"William Robert Arthur," she read, squinting to make out the words. "Born June 10, 1959, died June 11—oh, Harry, that's so sad!"

"Only a single day on this earth. One small boy, one small day." He levered himself backward and into a sitting position, his forearms resting on his knees as he stared at the stone. "I feel like a ghoul," he said, lowering his head. "Isn't there some other way?"

Suzi had pulled out a few weeds with shaking fingers, mindlessly doing some crude housekeeping of the small grave. "It's the only way, Harry. Wilbur says we apply for a new birth certificate in the name of—of William Robert Arthur," she said, her voice catching. "Then, when it arrives, we use it to get you all sorts of identification. A social security card, a driver's license—"

He laid a hand on her arm, stilling her in the process of tracing the carved "W" in "William" against the stone. "I'm sorry, Suzi. Sorry you ever got involved in this. But you're right. Wilbur's right. It's the only way."

Suzi sat on the deck chair at noon, staring into space, oblivious of her surroundings. For two weeks more she had kept Mrs. O'Reilly and Wilbur close to her, for protection, or so she told herself.

After all, she had invited a strange man into her house—a *very* strange man, indeed.

Just because he was bright, and amusing, and devastatingly handsome, didn't mean that she should be so trusting. Why, he could be a nineteenth-century version of Jack the Ripper. Or had Jack the Ripper actually lived in the nineteenth century? Yes, he had. Well, scratch that analogy.

Still, it simply wasn't prudent to be alone with Harry Wilde.

He was much too tempting.

And she was much too vulnerable to temptation.

Not that there had been a repeat of that mindblowing kiss the first night Wilbur had been in town. Oh, no. Suzi considered herself to be much too smart to get involved *that* way!

She had sent to *Literary Lines* the very next morning, requesting some galleys that she would be reviewing for the fall issue, and had done everything but closet herself in her bedroom for ten days, leaving Harry to blunder through conversations with a curiously unwilling-to-move Wilbur and to spend endless hours watching what Suzi had begun to term "that damned tele-vision machine."

If he asked her one more time if they could visit this wonderful place called "a theater near you," she was going to scream!

But for the past six days, since Wilbur had reluctantly left Ocean City—a place he had once said was only suitable for giggling toddlers and weary parents—and returned to Manhattan for the opening of a new art gallery, Harry had been transcribing his manuscript. He had written the original in his own form of code—or shorthand, as Suzi called his chicken scratches when she saw them—and had scarcely spoken to her.

Harry was a man with a mission, or so Mrs. O'Reilly had commented when she carried his untouched lunch tray up to the kitchen. The woman was right. When Harry watched television, he watched intently. When he played, he played intently.

But now, now that he was working on the thick manuscript that had been wrapped in oilskin and therefore had suffered little damage for its dunk in the Atlantic, he was like a man possessed.

Not that Suzi cared. She had her own work to do. Really. She couldn't have cared less if Harry never spoke to her again. If he never smiled at her in that silly, one-sided way of his. If he never touched her arm, or teased her, or walked hand in hand on the beach with her, or kissed her—

"Damn!"

"I so admire your clever way with words," Harry said from behind her, startling her into dropping the galley she had been reading without really comprehending, so that it slid off her lap to the floor, losing her place.

"Go away, Harry," she grumbled, not turning to look at him. After all, if she looked at him, if she saw his engaging smile, if she were to gaze into his laughing green-blue eyes, if she were to remember once again how very wonderful his arms had felt as he had held her close in their single embrace, their single kiss—well, if she were to keep remembering things like that it could be dangerous, that's all.

"If you insist, madam," he answered, his tone as well as his words mocking her. "I hear you older ladies can be a tad crotchety now and again."

"Harry Wilde!" Suzi exclaimed, turning so swiftly on the deck chair that it nearly tipped over. "You promised not to call me old ever again!"

"Hello, dear heart," he said, grinning, as she looked up at him. "It's not so difficult gaining your attention, if one only takes the time to go about the thing correctly. Would you like to read the mail that's just arrived? This one," he offered, holding up an official-looking envelope and waving it in front of her intriguingly, "might prove interesting."

"Your birth certificate!" She lunged for the envelope, grabbing it out of his hand. With trembling fingers she tore the envelope open and pulled out the certificate bearing the name William Robert Arthur. "Oh, Harry," she said, her nerves on edge as she leapt to her feet, "it's happening. You're on your way to becoming a whole new person."

He screwed up his face and scratched at a spot just behind his left ear, a habit that alerted her to the fact that he was going to say something she'd hate hearing. "Harry?" she prompted, replacing the certificate and clutching the envelope to her breasts.

"Would you care to take a stroll on the beach?" he asked, avoiding her eyes.

"No, I wouldn't," she answered warily. "I don't think that would be a good idea. You see, if you say something I don't like, I may be tempted to drown you."

"And Wilbur," Harry added, wincing.

"Wilbur? What's he got to do with anything?" Suzi didn't like the feeling she was getting in the pit of her stomach. It reminded her much too much of the feeling she'd had in her stomach that first morning, when Harry had told her it was 1813.

"First things first," he said taking her hand and quickly leading her toward the steps that led down to the path leading to the beach. "Let's walk, and let's talk about William Robert Arthur."

For all his insistence that he needed to speak with her, Harry kept curiously silent until they had traveled along the water's edge for some time, concentrating on kicking at the small wavelets that danced around their ankles.

Finally, just as she knew her nerves were about to tear—because he was still holding her hand—why did it affect her so much whenever he held her hand?—he said, "I can't become William Robert Arthur."

Suzi stopped dead, so that Harry was forced to halt as well or else chance having his arm torn out of its socket. "You can't *what?*"

He grinned at her. Oh, how dare he grin at her at a time like this?

"I said, I can't become William Rob—"

"For heaven's sake, don't repeat yourself. I heard you the first time, and it was bad enough then!" Suzi exploded, dropping his hand as if it might burn her. She then pushed the fingers of that hand through her hair and glared at him. "Harry Wilde, if I had a stick,

I'd hit you with it—repeatedly! *Why* can't you use the name?"

He stepped closer, so that his bare, fuzzy gold thighs were against her smooth skin, immediately giving her a panic attack of claustrophobia. "Because, Suzi Harper, I like the way you say 'Harry Wilde,'" he told her simply, resting his hands on her shoulders. "I like it exceedingly, and I should miss it. Very much."

"Oh, Harry," Suzi groaned, laying her head against his chest, not knowing whether to be angry or if she should burst into tears. "You stubborn, pigheaded, arrogant, wonderful Englishman. What in the world am I going to do with you?"

She heard the rumble of his soft laughter as she remained pressed against his chest. "Well, that brings us to Wilbur, doesn't it, dear heart?"

Suzi raised her head, unable to step away from him, because he was still holding fast to her shoulders. "It does? How?"

"Wilbur says that, to be safe, I should give serious thought to marrying myself an American citizen," Harry explained, his smile partly sheepish, partly intoxicating to her senses. "We've had several long talks on the subject and, although he still believes I am only an Englishman who has entered the country illegally, he was quite adamant about it."

"Marry an American citizen," Suzi repeated dully, her heart pounding so loudly she could barely hear herself speak. "But why? It isn't as if you were trying to get a Green Card—or whatever it is aliens need to live here and apply for citizenship. You'll be William Robert Arthur, and already a tax-paying citizen—if I can figure out what sort of job you could do, that is. I don't get it."

"I don't, either. Or at least I don't understand all of it. Wilbur says I'd be hedging my bets. If we attack the problem from two angles, we might just confuse the authorities if ever they decide to investigate me for any reason. That's when I realized, not unhappily, that we could confuse the authorities even more if I kept my own name. I could still remain your Harry Wilde."

At last Suzi succeeded in moving away from Harry, which might not have been a good idea, for her head was spinning and she wouldn't be surprised if she toppled headfirst onto the beach. "Marry. Keep your own name."

She looked at him quizzically, realizing that she was still holding the birth certificate, had been carrying it with her along the beach without realizing it. "But how would we change the name on this?" she asked, waving the badly creased envelope in front of her.

He lifted her chin with his hand and dropped a kiss on the tip of her nose, a move that turned her knees to limp seaweed. "Wilbur is convinced you're an inventive puss. You'll think of some way," he said, taking her hand once more and leading her back up the beach toward the condo.

"Oh, yeah. Right. Suzi will think of something. Suzi has larceny in her soul. No wonder he went back to Manhattan. He knew I'd go nuclear if he'd dared to suggest such a thing in person! Tell me, Harry, did Wilbur make any 'suggestions' as to where you're going to find this willing American citizen who'll marry you just so you won't be deported to oblivion one fine day? You can't go back to England, you know. You're not a man without a country—you're a man without a *century!*''

Who would Harry marry? As if there could be any other woman—not counting Mrs. O'Reilly, of course. As soon as the question was out of her mouth Suzi had longed to take it back. Of course Wilbur had had a woman in mind. The sneak! That wonderful, romantic, mischief-making *sneak!* The man plays Cupid for his son-in-law, then Courtney, then Countney's daughter, Sydney—and now he thinks he's got a corner on the market.

They had reached the outside steps when Harry finally answered her question. ''Wilbur suggested you, naturally,'' he said, stepping aside so that she could precede him up to the deck. ''And that's when I first knew I was right to want to keep my own name—the moment Wilbur tried the name Suzi Wilde out loud and then asked me if I thought that it should be considered a name or a description.''

''I hate you,'' Suzi declared feelingly as she turned at the top of the steps and glared down at him. ''I hate you, I hate Wilbur, I hate men in general. You in particular, but all men in general. Is that clear?''

''Partially. Would that be a 'no' then, Miss Harper?'' Harry asked, his wide, infuriating grin revealing his confidence in her answer.

And it was that confidence that made her balk. ''How do you know I'm not in love with someone? For all you know I might be in love with a half-dozen men! Or didn't that occur to you?''

"You?" Harry appeared to be amazed, and then he grinned. "I would have thought you were past the age for—"

"Don't you finish that sentence, Harry Wilde," Suzi threatened. "Don't you even *think* it!"

"I wouldn't dare, madam," Harry answered, so that she knew he was deliberately teasing her, trying to make the moment easier on them both. Harry was a dear man, really he was. And he'd be lost without her. Absolutely lost.

But he didn't love her. He had never mentioned, or even hinted, at the word *love.*

There was a short, uncomfortable silence between them before Harry asked, "So, all things considered, and realizing that I am asking you to sacrifice that freedom you modern women so cherish—should I take your lack of answer as a 'no'?"

"Yes, damn it! I mean, *no!* I'll marry you." She held out her hands in warning as he moved to take her in his arms. "But only because you'd be totally helpless without me, Harry Wilde—and because it's the best way I can think of to make your life a misery!"

And with that she was off, running for the condo and the safety of her bedroom.

Chapter Six

Harry had been in his bedroom working on transcribing his manuscript when Suzi had called for him to join her in the foyer. Something in her voice, a bubbling enthusiasm not unmixed with wonder, told him he was about to be amazed. He didn't know if he was going to be *happy,* but he was going to be amazed. Suzie Harper constantly amazed him.

He wasn't disappointed.

He was amazed, and he wasn't happy.

Suzi Harper, a strange young woman he was fast beginning to believe was the mother of all invention, had tossed his precious, bogus birth certificate into the fully loaded washing machine!

"I first got the idea while looking at the certificate, and saw how it was all creased from the way I had been holding it," Suzi explained as they stood in the foyer, the open bifold doors that usually concealed the automatic clothes washer and dryer behind her.

The clothes washer was in the process of its spin cycle now, or so Suzi had informed him a moment ago when he had closed his gaping mouth and decided he could listen to her without throttling her, and Harry could feel his nerves tightening, wondering what sort of dastardly crime he had committed in his lifetime to be punished in this bizarre way.

"You see, Harry," Suzi was saying, "I've often left something, sometimes a piece of paper—sometimes a couple of dollars—in my pocket, so that it ended up going through the washer. Even the dryer, once or twice. It makes a hell of a mess."

He was beginning to understand, not that he put much credence in her belief that her plan would work. "But will it cover up the fact that you changed William Robert Arthur to Harry Wilde? That white liquid you painted over the original name was quite magical, but a discerning eye could still see that the certificate has been altered."

"Oh, ye of little faith!" Suzi exclaimed as the washing machine gave a small click, a slight sigh, and slowed to a stop. "It'll work just fine. Trust me."

"It would appear I do not have any other option, doesn't it?" Harry said, leaning against the curved banister of the spiral staircase and wishing he could will himself to be stern. But it was difficult not to be infused with Suzi's almost childlike optimism.

She tipped back the lid and reached into the washing machine, giving Harry a delightful picture of her long legs peeping out beneath her bright pink short-

shorts. He did the gentlemanly thing, and turned away, then gave into temptation and indulged himself in admiring the view.

They were going to be married.

And optimism was optimism.

His luck hadn't been unremittingly bad.

Three days had passed since Suzi had accepted his ramshackle proposal of marriage, two of those days spent mostly in uncomfortable silences interspersed with covert looks and nervous smiles. Suzi had concentrated on her own work and he had walked the beach, unable to focus on transcribing more than a few pages of his manuscript before his mind returned to thoughts of Suzi and their upcoming nuptials.

A marriage of convenience. An accepted practice in his time, perhaps, but not in hers. Americans most especially married for love, and only for love. Not for convenience. Not for money. Not for titles or position. And most definitely not to obtain an identity.

But Wilbur had been adamant. He had vowed that the only surefire way to elude detection was to marry an American citizen. Wilbur had said that Suzi should settle down, that marriage might be the making of her, and that her "biological clock," whatever that was, was ticking away at a mighty pace, and if there was ever a woman who should be surrounded by her own children it was Suzi Harper.

Children. Harry raised one eyebrow as he watched Suzi searching through the small collection of wet beach towels, on the lookout for the birth certificate.

Would there be children?

A better question.

Would there be love?

There was already desire, on his part.

There was already compassion, on hers.

Could there be more? Could he believe, trust, in the promise of more?

"Ta-da! Mission accomplished. Harry—come look!"

He shook his head, trying to clear it of questions, those never-ending questions that had kept him from his rest these past two nights, and obediently pinned a bright smile on his face. "You've wrought a miracle, Suzi?" he asked, taking the soggy paper from her.

There were several fold marks visible, and the paper was dangerously delicate in its saturated condition, but it was still legible—if you looked carefully. What was missing was the former pristine white newness of the paper, so that Suzi's alterations were no longer apparent.

He looked at her in genuine admiration. "Have you ever considered counterfeiting as an avocation, dear heart?" he asked, watching her as she tried without noticeable success to hide her elation in this latest victory. "I believe you might have a true calling to larceny."

"What can I say, Harry?" she asked, skipping past him, her grin devilish. "You bring out the worst in me. Now, come on. We have to shower and dress while the certificate dries. We were just lucky I could have my own certificate expressed here from Manhattan in time. The local licensing office closes at four and won't open again until Monday. There's a three-day waiting period for marriages, you know, and we still have to get our blood tests.''

Harry stood very still for a moment, considering her words, and feeling his feet slowly going numb. ''Blood—blood tests?'' He'd been examining the television machine late last night when he couldn't sleep, using the remote control to ''channel-surf,'' as Suzi condemned the practice which she decried as having something to do with his male genes and not the century in which he was born.

At three o'clock in the morning he'd discovered a channel devoted to subjects in a medical vein—vein? was he going to be required to open a vein?—and had watched a heart transplant surgery in mingled horror and fascination until he could summon the power to click to another channel.

Modern medicine made submitting himself to the quacks and leeches and tooth-drawers of nineteenth-century England seem preferable to anything the modern world had conjured up in the name of ''progress.''

''Um—Suzi?'' he ventured, clearing his throat. ''Precisely what is a blood test? How do they test it? For what perverted, ungodly purpose do they test it? And lastly, and most definitely most important to my peace of mind—how do they acquire this blood in the first place?''

Suzi turned in the act of entering her bedroom and looked at him quizzically. And then she grinned. It was an evil grin. She held up her hands in front of her, about a foot apart. ''How do they get it, Harry? Why, it's simple. They use a needle—about *this* long!''

Harry knew she was enjoying herself at his expense, but could not keep from asking, "What sort of needle? A sewing needle? A knitting needle?"

"I don't believe this!" Suzi exclaimed upstairs fifteen nauseating minutes later, after she had instructed him in the ways of modern bloodletting—using drawings to explain her explanation. "You're whiter now than when I fished you out of the ocean. Harry, it's only a small needle, and it only pinches for a second. Honestly. I wouldn't lie to you."

"Yes, you would," Harry said firmly, his arms folded against him, protecting the vulnerable crooks of his elbows. He'd never been ill a day in his life—except for that embarrassing bout with measles when he was fifteen—but he'd seen physicians in action, and knew he'd rather face an entire fleet of American warships than submit himself to their ministrations. "Not only would you lie to me, but you'd enjoy yourself while you were about it. Have you ever had one of these blood tests?"

"Everyone has, Harry," she told him as she led the way to the spiral staircase once more, her tone shifting from amusement to exasperation. "Don't worry. I'll go first, and you can watch me. All right? Now hurry up. If we don't go through with this now I may get cold feet."

"The thought of marrying me is that daunting?" Harry asked, forgetting the coming horror of the blood test as his attention was once more brought back to the fact that Suzi was marrying him, but for all the wrong reasons.

"No, silly," she told him, once more heading for her bedroom. "As an old maid more likely to be struck by lightning than to find a husband, I'm getting rather used to the idea of being a wife. It's the clerk in the licensing office I'm worried about. If we can't pull this off this afternoon, Harry, I'll be spending the next few years in jail. And I don't even want to *think* about what might happen to you! I saw a movie once where scientists discovered a mermaid on land and wanted to dissect her!"

One short hour later Harry was to remember Suzi's words as they stood on the other side of the counter from a rather overwhelming, overbearing woman in her early sixties who insisted upon staring him down overtop her heavy gold-rimmed reading glasses as if he had just recently crawled out from beneath a nearby rock.

"Don't you know how important this paper is, Mr. Wilde?" the clerk asked him accusingly, gingerly holding on to the still-damp certificate with her fingertips, as if it might contaminate her in some way.

"Indeed, madam, I do," Harry answered earnestly, and in his best schoolboy English. "But I was so in a rush to marry Miss Harper here that I inadvertently left the certificate in my trousers and her housekeeper placed them both in the washing machine. I—" he continued, inventively, he thought, when she continued to glare at him "—I have been carrying the certificate with me for weeks, in the fervent hope Miss Harper would honor my suit."

He put an arm around Suzi, drawing her stiff, tense body close against his. "When my dearest heart finally agreed to the marriage, my elation must have done war with my common sense, and lost the battle." He smiled at the clerk, hoping to dazzle her. He'd always had a way with older ladies.

Except for this one.

"If you were born in New Jersey, what are you doing with that English accent?"

"Harry's parents were diplomats, and traveled extensively. He was educated at Oxford," Suzi explained proudly—and rather quickly—as she gazed up at him adoringly, her fib much more convincing than his, he thought meanly. "Weren't you, my darling?" Then she, too, looked to the clerk and added in a near whisper, "I believe the man exaggerates his accent to impress me, but I don't care. I think it's adorable! Don't you think it's *absolutely* adorable?"

The clerk sniffed, clearly less "impressed" than Suzi with Harry's accent. Then she inspected the certificate again before placing it on the counter and picking up a pen and glaring at Harry. "Occupation?"

"Lieutenant, His Maj—"

"Freelance writer!" Suzi fairly screamed, effectively drowning out his verbal slip as she delivered a sharp, painful kick to his ankle.

"Writer, is it?" the woman scoffed. "So's my brother-in-law, who's been sponging off my sister Winifred these thirty-some odd years. How about I put down unemployed? It's the same thing."

Longing to reach across the counter and cuff the woman's ears—an action that would probably end badly—Harry only smiled and nodded his head.

"Social security number?"

Harry and Suzi exchanged horrified glances. He didn't have a social security number. They hadn't thought he'd need it simply to get married.

It was Suzi who came to the rescue again, rattling off a series of numbers Harry knew she was making up as she went along, and the clerk scribbled on the form once more.

"Can't he speak for himself?" the woman asked, pointing her pen at Harry.

"Suzi believes me incapable of dealing with anything the slightest bit numerical," he offered in explanation. "And she's correct, of course. You know how it is with people of an artistic bent—we have no head for mundane, everyday matters."

"You can say that again," the clerk agreed grudgingly. "Winifred's husband couldn't find his own way home from the corner market at high noon. This your birth certificate?" she asked, taking the paper Suzi offered her. "Well, at least I can read this one."

"This isn't going well," Suzi whispered out of the corner of her mouth as the older woman turned to a table behind her to pick up another form. "I think she's on to us, Harry."

"On to us? You mean, she suspects something is wrong? How?"

Suzi tugged on his arm, moving him three steps back from the counter. "I don't know how. Just keep your mouth shut and let me handle her. Okay?"

Harry was beginning to feel extremely frustrated, and not a little out of his depth. He didn't want Suzi to "handle" the situation. He, after all, was the man, the strong one. He would be the one to save them, if they needed to be saved. He'd show the woman that he was as American as she was!

He shook off Suzi's hand and returned to the counter as the clerk picked up her pen once more, obviously ready to ask another penetrating, hard to answer question.

"How 'bout them Phillies?" he piped up in imitation of the rather sloppy grammar of the gas station attendant he'd seen on one of his rare outings, briskly slapping his hand against the counter, calling on his scant reserves of knowledge about the major league baseball team he'd been watching perform on television. "Dropping three in a row to St. Louis! They're going to blow the pennant if they keep this up."

"I don't like sports. As a matter of fact, I *detest* sports," the woman said crushingly, her beady brown eyes narrowing. "Charlie, my ex-husband, liked sports. The little squirt watched sports night and day. Baseball. Hockey. Football. Basketball. Anything with a ball, or a hoop, or a goal. That's *why* he's my ex-husband, and why I'm standing here earning my own keep rather than working in my garden."

She turned to Suzi and wagged a finger at her. "You'd better rethink this, little girl, if your fiancé is anything like my ex. Take my word as gospel on this one—he'll break your heart."

Suzi flashed Harry a triumphant smile. "Oh, but he's so *cute!*" she exclaimed, launching herself at him, sliding her arms up and around his neck and lifting her feet off the ground, so that he nearly stumbled. "Isn't he cute?" And then, as she literally hung suspended from his neck, and to Harry's mingled surprise and pleasure, she kissed him.

"Dear heart," he said in all sincerity long moments later as he attempted to catch his breath.

"Sweet darling," Suzi crooned with syrupy sweetness, running one hand through the long hair that lay against his nape. "My own little sugar snookums. Look at him! So cute! So cute, so cute, *so cute!* Oh, I can barely wait until we're married. I simply can't keep my hands off this gorgeous hunk of man another minute! I'm *crazy* about him!"

"Crazy? A mutual condition, I agree," Harry said, nuzzling her throat as she molded her small, delightful body against him.

He didn't know what she was doing, but he wasn't so bacon-brained that he was about to push her away and demand an explanation. Not while she was pressing short, hot kisses on his cheeks, his mouth, and going on and on about the romantic heart-shaped hot tub to be found at their honeymoon cottage in a place called the Poconos.

Only vaguely did he hear the mad frenzy of stamping behind him as the clerk placed official seals on the small pile of documents on the counter. "Here!" she then exclaimed nervously, her voice fairly trembling with disgust. "Take these and get out of my office."

Suzi whispered in his ear, which was a simple matter of logistics, for she happened to be nibbling on it at the time. "Pick me up and aim me toward the counter," she instructed, her breath warm against his neck.

He was almost beyond hearing her. He had, in fact, almost forgotten where they were, why they were there and even who he was. All he could concentrate on was Suzi's mouth, Suzi's roaming hands, Suzi's ardor.

But, somehow, he managed to respond to her order. Suzi relaxed her grip on him long enough to scoop up the papers and, a moment later, they were heading for the door, Suzi still held high against his chest and gurgling, "Oh, yes, Harry. *Yes!* Take me home! *Now!*"

"…just about the most disgusting display I've ever witnessed in all my born days," the clerk was muttering as they exited the licensing office. "I get them all in here! Can't tell whether to issue the idiots a license or throw a bucket of cold water over the pair of them. Why, in my day…"

Much to Harry's confusion and regret, once the door was closed behind them Suzi's ardor abruptly cooled and she wriggled out of his arms just as he was about to kiss her once more. "Thanks for going along with me, *sugar snookums,*" she said, fumbling with the papers as she attempted to locate the all-important marriage license application.

Then she smoothed down her fairly rumpled lime green blouse in a coolly businesslike "that's that" demonstration of dismissal and grinned up at him impishly. "I thought that went quite well, didn't you? She couldn't wait to get rid of us and our embarrassing display of libido."

Harry believed he could feel Charlie's ex-wife's bucket of cold water pouring over his head and all over his "libido." So Suzi's little exhibition had all been for effect? He took a deep, steadying breath and willed his features into a noncommittal expression. Of course Suzi had been only putting on an act, playing a part. He knew that. He'd known it all along. Now, if he could only control his ragged breathing.

"Are we legal now?" he asked, looking down at the papers.

She shook her head as they made their way back to the parking lot and Suzi's car. "Not yet. Once we have the blood test results I'll have to come back here one more time and get the final papers. You don't have to come along for that, thank goodness, or we might have to repeat our performance if the dragon lady is on duty."

"Yes. That would be tragic, wouldn't it." Harry stepped in front of Suzi as she went to walk around to her side of the car. "Was that all it was back there, Suzi? A performance?"

"What else would it be, Harry?" she asked, looking in his direction, but not directly at him. "We both know why we're doing this. I rescued you, so in a way, I'm responsible for you. We're stuck with each other, unless you plan to announce to the world that you've traveled through time. We have to live together, so we might as well be married. Left on your own you'd be a menace to society and yourself. Harry, we've been over all of this already."

"Yes, of course," Harry agreed, watching her as she went around the car and opened the driver's side door. Her reasoning was good, but her voice lacked conviction. He took heart in that thought. "Although I won't lie and say I didn't enjoy the exercise,

sugar snookums," he ended daringly as she was about
to slide onto the seat.

"Oh, Harry!" Suzi exclaimed in what he decided
was nervous exasperation, her head hastily disap-
pearing into the car, so that he quickly got in himself
and watched her as she struggled with the seat belt,
doing his best to look sheepish and appealing at the
same time.

"Oh, Harry!" he parroted, smiling as a becoming
tide of pink rose into her cheeks, then settled back in
his seat. "And, *oh, Suzi!*"

She started the car, staring daggers at him, and
pulled out into traffic, a move that still chilled him to
the bone. Although his former idea of speed had been
pleasantly shattered with his first drive in Suzi's car,
he knew he would feel more comfortable with the
reins—the wheel—and his life, in his hands rather than
in those of a mere female who should be sitting beside
him, gushingly complimenting him on his expertise.

"I'll just bet the laboratory technician will be able
to wipe that self-satisfied smirk off your face," Suzi
told him, turning into another parking lot located beside a building labeled Medical Laboratory.

"Ah, yes," he countered smugly, for he was still
feeling rather smug. After all, a woman who truly de-
tested him would have found some other way of di-
verting the clerk than by throwing herself in his arms
and therefore throwing convention to the four winds!
"But I am equally convinced that you will be able to
kiss away my pain."

"I hate you, Harry Wilde," Suzi declared as she
slammed the car door.

"No, you don't," Harry said, taking her hand as they made their way to the front door of the office building. "You seem to delight in saying so, but you don't hate me. As a matter of fact, I believe we are rubbing along together tolerably well. We certainly *rubbed* together to advantage in front of that most delightful clerk. Ours should be an interesting marriage, don't you think?"

"Shut up, Harry," Suzi ordered. "Just do us both a favor and shut up." However, he noticed with a happy, hopeful heart, she did not let go of his hand.

Suzi relaxed on the lounge chair, the cares of the day behind her as she watched the stars appearing one by one in the clear, darkening sky.

If only the worries of tomorrow, those of all her tomorrows once she and Harry were married, could disappear as simply.

For tomorrow she and Harry Wilde would be married. Irrevocably joined. Man and woman, husband and wife, time traveler and flighty female.

Only she wasn't flighty. She wasn't! *Quixotic.* That's what she was. And Harry was lucky to have found her. Who else would have believed the man had traveled through time—yet alone helped him cover his tracks by marrying him? Only her, that's who. The quixotic Suzi Harper.

She sighed, looking out over the ocean, listening as the waves broke against the beach below, and remembering that embarrassing, enlightening scene in the clerk's office. "How 'bout them Phillies?" Could he have been any more transparent? How had the absurd idea of kissing Harry to keep him from saying anything else entered her head? And, better yet, why had she acted on the impulse?

Harry had to know now that she was not indifferent to him. Indifferent? Hah! She was fascinated by him. He was handsome. He was intelligent and endlessly curious. He was very handsome. He was sweet, and polite, and kind, and very, *very* handsome.

Good grief! She was hooked. Why didn't she just admit it to herself, even if she'd die before she told Harry how very much she wanted to be married to him.

Married. Tomorrow. In less than twenty-four hours. Suzi Wilde. Suzanne Wilde. Mrs. Harry Wilde. *Oh, Lord!*

All their plans had already been made, not that there were many of them. It would be a small wedding in a small town away from prying eyes, a legally binding ceremony before the justice of the peace and with Mrs. O'Reilly as their sole witness.

Suzi supposed she should be grateful for "small" favors. She had never wanted a large wedding anyway, although anyone who thought they knew her would most certainly be excused if they imagined otherwise.

But, for all her love of pomp, she had always imagined her marriage to be a very private thing, perhaps with her vows being whispered in a shady glen, with only the minister, her soon-to-be husband and the birds in the trees to hear them.

Besides, she decided with a rueful smile, how could they possibly have a large wedding? Who'd sit on the groom's side, for pity's sake? And another thing. She wouldn't have to be made nervous by the obligatory weekend visit to meet Harry's relatives. That would have been an impossibly long trip, wouldn't it?

Suzi's small smile turned into a wide grin, and soon she was giggling, which was a good thing, because anyone who might stumble out onto the deck would mistake her tears for those of mirth.

But, then, didn't all brides cry before their weddings?

Harry stood on the moonlit beach, his hands stuffed deep in the pockets of his rolled up white-duck trousers, his long blond hair blown around by the sea breeze, his bare feet being lapped at gently by the small wavelets that crept along the sand at the water's edge.

He'd be married in the morning. Married to Suzanne Harper. His rescuer. His mentor. The thorn in his side. The angel in his dreams. The woman who had offered so much, sacrificed so much and asked for so little in return.

How could he do this to her? How could he allow her to throw her life away on a man she barely knew, a man who had only recently come to her from a world so different from hers he might as well have landed here after half a lifetime on some distant planet?

How would he support her? With his writings? Did Suzi's world care about the adventures and musings of a nineteenth-century dreamer turned reluctant soldier in a war he neither believed in nor could turn his back on and still call himself a man?

Would a man live on the largess of his wife? Many of his contemporaries had done so, and bragged about it. But not him. Not Harry Wilde! He'd have to find a way to support Suzi. Support their children.

Their children. Harry sighed, watching as the movement of the ocean turned the path of moonlight shining down on it into a fragile stairway to the heavens. It was terribly romantic, this Ocean City beach. But he was out here alone, and Suzi was avoiding him.

Suzi knew what their marriage tomorrow would mean. Neither of them had said the words, but they both knew. This would be a marriage of convenience—even of necessity—but it would not be a marriage in name only.

Suzi deserved children. She deserved love and honor and loyalty. She deserved kindness, and gentleness, and the sweet romance all women seemed to crave, all of which had been glaringly missing in their relationship thus far.

He couldn't go to her, tell her he loved her, and have any chance of being believed. He wouldn't believe it, either, for their association was still too new, too bizarre, to really know much of anything. But he did care for Suzi. He cared for her deeply. He desired her.

He wouldn't rush her, he wouldn't too assiduously pursue the blossoming of mutual trust, the mutual—he was sure—desire, the promise of mutual love. It would all come to them, in time.

Time. Was it their friend, or their enemy? If only he could suppress the feeling that there was something potentially dangerous about his strange voyage to the twentieth century that still alluded him. Some future problem he wasn't seeing.

He picked up a flat, broken seashell and sent it skipping across the waves.

He wouldn't think about problems now.

After all, he should be happy, on top of the world. He was getting married in the morning.

Chapter Seven

Suzi, who couldn't remember ever being upset with the long-suffering Mrs. O'Reilly, felt close to shaking the woman. She had been dawdling, and delaying, and offering one lame excuse after another as Suzi attempted to get her to the front door of the condo.

"Wait!" Mrs. O'Reilly said now, just as Suzi thought she had settled all the housekeeper's questions and opened the front door in anticipation of the three of them leaving for the office of the justice of the peace.

"Now what?" Suzi complained. "And don't tell me you have another run in your stocking, Mrs. O'Reilly, because I don't care if you do. The justice of the peace is waiting for us—if he hasn't retired and moved to Florida after giving up on us, that is."

"Perhaps she's politely showing us that she doesn't wish to bear witness to the ceremony?" Harry suggested, broadly winking at a becomingly disconcerted Mrs. O'Reilly before turning to once more inspect his appearance in the mirror beside the door.

He had been admiring himself all morning, Suzi knew. And she didn't blame him. He was gorgeous to look at in his new double-breasted suit, the sort of man who was born to wear designer clothes as naturally as some men wore jeans and T-shirts.

"No, no, Mr. Wilde. It's nothing like that, as well you know, you scamp. I've grown rather fond of you, you know." Mrs. O'Reilly turned and headed for the spiral staircase once more as Suzi silently and incredulously mouthed the words "you scamp" under her breath. "But I think I may have left the kettle on the boil. That would never do, would it? Can't go burning down this lovely house, especially when you consider that I've just scrubbed it from top to bottom. I'll be right back, Miss Harper, I promise."

"Where have I heard that before?" Suzi groused, rolling her eyes. "Oh, I give up!"

"Morning, all. Quite the perfect day for a wedding, isn't it? The drive from Manhattan was glorious, if a bit delayed by a last-minute errand."

"Wilbur, come in, " Harry said in greeting, not looking at all surprised by the publisher's appearance in the doorway. "Lovely to see you again, dear man. Once more you have put my own attempts at sartorial splendor firmly in the shade. My compliments to your tailor."

"Hallelujah! Er, that is, never mind about the kettle, Miss Harper. I remember now—I turned it off just after breakfast," Mrs. O'Reilly piped up happily, and in obvious relief, as Wilbur Langley strolled through the doorway and into the foyer, his uniformed chauffeur following after him, carrying an enormous white box decorated with a huge pink ribbon.

The housekeeper brushed close by Wilbur as she relieved the chauffeur of his burden, and whispered to the two men, "My stars, what I've been through trying to keep her in one place! I thought you'd *never* get here," and with a heavy sigh, headed for Suzi's bedroom.

Suzi shook her head. It didn't take a rocket scientist to figure out that, although Mrs. O'Reilly might be on her payroll, she had been working for Wilbur Langley for at least these past few weeks. "Wilbur, you're impossible, incorrigible and a bit of a traitor, now that I think about it," she said without anger, going up on tiptoe to kiss his cheek.

"Yes, I am, rather, aren't I?" The publisher turned to Harry and the two men shook hands, each equally happy to see the other. "Now that I've played deliveryman, you won't mind if I come along to give the bride away, will you, Harry?"

"I should be delighted, sir," Harry responded, his sea blue eyes twinkling. "I hope it wasn't too much of a bother, procuring my bridal gift? I shall reimburse you from my gaming winnings, as promised. Was it very difficult to have my design implemented?"

"Not at all. The seamstress had no problem, or so she assured me. I haven't yet seen it, but I am convinced everything went well."

Now Suzi was confused. Had Mrs. O'Reilly phoned Wilbur in Manhattan and spilled the beans, or had Harry? "I didn't know you'd mastered long-distance dialing, Harry," she said, part of her wanting to know everything that had been going on behind her back, and another part of her longing to rip into the big white box and see her unexpected present. She didn't know what it was, but it was bound to be beautiful. Both Wilbur and Harry had excellent taste!

"Oh, yes," Harry answered calmly. "And just the other day, the overnight mails and the fax machine as well. Mrs. O'Reilly has been endlessly helpful."

Suzi bristled, forgetting the present. "Anyone in skirts wants to be 'endlessly helpful' to you, you sneak. So the two of you have been running around behind my back, carrying tales to Wilbur? Why aren't I surprised? You and Wilbur might have been cut from the same bolt of natural fiber silk! What was the fax for?"

"To send me the sketch of his requirements for your bridal gown, of course," Wilbur told her, taking her by the elbow and guiding her toward her bedroom. "Not that you don't look lovely in the ensemble you have chosen, my pet—a *Donna Karan* unless I miss my guess. Now why don't you be a good little bride? Toddle off and allow Mrs. O'Reilly to assist you in dressing. We're already running late, you know."

"My—my wedding gown?" She looked to Wilbur, who was making shooing motions in her direction, and then to Harry, who was standing there looking so maddeningly innocent, so adorable.

Suzi was going to cry. She just knew it. She was going to stand here and start blubbering like some emotional baby, making a complete fool of herself. "Harry, you bought me a wedding gown?"

"It's not the more traditional bridal gift of pearls, I agree, dear heart," Harry said rather formally, as if he, as well as she, was suddenly operating under some emotional strain. "However, I felt the need to indulge myself in a small fantasy. You will, I hope, do me the pleasure of honoring my wishes in this matter."

Indulge a small fantasy? What had Harry meant by that? "I suppose so," Suzi told him hesitantly, looking to Wilbur, hoping something in his expression would tell her whether Harry's gift would delight or dismay her. "As long as there isn't a spinster's cap or some such English monstrosity in that box."

"Oh, for shame, Suzi," Wilbur said in slightly bored tones, pulling back his French cuff to glance at his gold Rolex. "Time's a-wasting, my dear. Go after Mrs. O'Reilly. You can be impolite to us all again later if you feel the need."

Knowing when she was beaten, and now more interested than ever in seeing the contents of the box, Suzi gave up the fight and returned to her bedroom, only taking time to slam the door to show that she didn't much like being ordered around like a misbehaving child.

"Oh, my goodness!" she exclaimed as she slowly walked across the room to the bed, where Mrs.

'O'Reilly was lifting the gown from a small mountain of tissue paper. "It's lovely!"

The gown was simply made of some sort of soft, natural fabric, a pattern of extremely tiny, delicately stemmed purple flowers scattered across a white background. The neck of the gown was a modest scoop, the design high-waisted, banded just below her breasts by a thin purple velvet ribbon, then flowing softly down to ankle-length, where it ended in a small ruffle much like those that edged the short, cap sleeves.

"There's gloves, lovely white satin shoes in your size and a bonnet the likes of which I haven't seen since I was a girl in Brooklyn and my mother bought us all new bonnets for Easter-time. I think we should pile your hair up high on your head, the way you did for that dinner at the Metropolitan Museum last winter, and well—Miss Harper, I think you should see this for yourself," Mrs. O'Reilly said, holding out a small velvet box.

"Thank you, Mrs. O'Reilly," Suzi said absently as she took the jeweler's box, still staring at the gown. Harry wanted her to look like a Regency Miss, if that was the correct term for a young lady of his time. He wasn't insulting her; he was indulging in a "small fantasy." The gesture was sweet, touching and very revealing. Harry was treating her as if she was his affianced wife, and not just the woman circumstance was forcing him to marry.

Now she knew she was going to cry.

She became aware that she was holding the jeweler's box and snapped it open to see Harry's signet ring inside. He had been wearing it the day he'd voyaged through time and into her life, but she didn't remember seeing it on his hand this past week.

The ring was solid gold, a small, elaborately curved and swirling *W* engraved on its small oval surface. How had it come to be in with the gown Wilbur had brought from Manhattan? Oh, yes. Harry had "mastered" the overnight mails, hadn't he?

She lifted the ring from its velvet bed and experimentally slipped it onto the third finger of her left hand. It fit perfectly.

"I sent along one of your own rings in the same box, so Mr. Langley could get it sized right," Mrs. O'Reilly explained, dabbing at her eyes before loudly blowing her nose. "Isn't it lovely? Mr. Wilde has been planning this for more than a week. It's like something out of a fairy tale, that's what it is. Isn't Mr. Wilde the most romantic, considerate man you ever met?"

Suzi looked up at the housekeeper, so blinded by tears she could barely make out the woman's broadly grinning face.

It took the better part of an hour for Wilbur to satisfy himself as to the arrangement of the small truckload of flowers he'd ordered for the justice of the peace's shabby living room, excluding the time he'd spent rehearsing the justice's wife as she played that old sentimental standard, "Because," on her out-of-tune piano.

During that time, the happy couple had been told to amuse themselves as best they could. Suzi, who had barely spoken except to shyly thank Harry for his gifts, had asked to sit alone in the office.

Harry, not sure if Suzi was avoiding him or merely playing the bride who should not risk bad luck by seeing the groom too close to the ceremony, paced the small, depressingly brown garden behind the justice's office.

As he paced, he tried to tell himself it was only natural that he should have been shocked spitless by Suzi's appearance. The gown had worked like a magician's trick, seemingly transporting him back to Mayfair and the world he had left. A world he had thought to see again if he did not die in battle. A world he knew now he would never see again.

Suzi, by the simple act of donning that gown and its complementing straw bonnet, would have dazzled London society with her presence! Blond, petite, with skin as pure and smooth as marble, and with blue eyes as large and guileless as Caroline Lamb's, she would have taken the town by storm, becoming the sensation of the Season.

Why, if Suzi Harper had been a debutante in 1813, he wouldn't have gotten within fifty yards of her, having been cut out by every titled gentleman who could pen an ode to her eyelashes or dazzle her with his box at the opera.

If Suzi Harper had been a debutante in 1813, he might never have been able to do more than worship her from afar as she went down the dance at Almack's, then retire to his club to drown his sorrows in a bottle.

But Suzi Harper was not a debutante and this was not 1813. All thoughts of London, of his past life, receded without another moment's regret. For Suzi Harper was here, as was he, they were about to be married—and Harry felt more nervous than if he were some green as grass looby straight from the country about to face his first evening in London society.

Would Wilbur ever be done fussing and stage-managing the business so that they could get on with the ceremony? Much as he admired the man for his many talents and appreciated his gift of the flowers, Harry knew he was within seconds of bodily removing Wilbur Langley from the scene so that the justice of the peace could pronounce the vows and have done with it!

At last Mrs. O'Reilly opened the back door and loudly "Yoo-hooed" at Harry, motioning for him to come inside. Harry took a deep breath, collected his composure and followed the housekeeper into the living room, doing his best not to laugh at the woman's choice of headgear—a small box of a hat decorated with a single red rose that insisted upon jiggling up and down with every heavy tread of her sensible-shoe clad feet.

Wilbur had wrought a miracle, turning the small living room into a woodland glen, more than a dozen tall, leafy plants bordered by baskets of daisies, and violets, and white-as-snow roses obscuring any sight of the furnishings.

The justice of the peace stood beneath a ceiling-high horseshoe-shaped white wooden trellis that was dripping with wisteria much the same shade as the violet flowers in Suzi's gown. And, much to Harry's quiet amusement, it appeared that the man's suit had only recently been pressed, his gravy-stained tie replaced by a clean one.

"You're to stand over here, Mr. Wilde," Mrs. O'Reilly told him, waving him to the right of the trellis with the hand that clutched a bouquet of daisies. "That's it. I have to go into the other room, then come out again, just like a real matron of honor. It was Mr. Langley's idea. Now, don't go away."

"I wouldn't think of it, madam," he said, grinning as the justice's wife began murdering the piano. It was nice to learn that Wilbur wasn't infallible.

And then Harry didn't think much of anything at all, because Mrs. O'Reilly appeared once more—minus the rose-topped hat—her wide Irish face beaming as she took the scant half-dozen short strides that brought her to the trellis. She stepped carefully to one side, then turned to look back at the doorway, and Harry followed suit.

Suzi entered on Wilbur's arm, dressed as he'd already seen her, but now wearing the bonnet and carrying a nosegay of violets, her eyes demurely downcast. The baby's breath nestled among the violets trembled because her hand was trembling... because she was nervous... because she was about to throw her life away on a man she only recently had met but could not avoid... had bravely decided she could not allow to face his new, unknown, unknowing world on his own.

Harry wanted to run, to take himself off before Suzi could sacrifice herself, before she was eternally bound to him, a man she did not know, could not love. At the same time he wanted to be a gentleman—be a man!—and refuse to give in to this sudden madness that told him that if he ran from Suzi Harper now he would be the biggest coward in eternity.

And then Suzi raised her gaze, saw the towering green plants, saw the flowers, saw the trellis—saw Harry.

She saw them all.

And she smiled through the tears standing in her eyes.

"Wilbur, how did you know?"

"I pride myself on knowing everything, my pet," he answered, finishing his last bite of wedding cake in the small private dining room he had hired for the postwedding luncheon. "However, if you are referring to my decorations for the ceremony, I would remind you that you were rather vocal on the subject after dear Sydney's lavish affair last fall."

Suzi averted her eyes. "That's right," she said, blushing. "I had a few glasses of wine that day, didn't I? It was wonderful—watching Courtney's daughter walk down the aisle—but a little scary as well. I mean, when my friends' children are getting married and I'm still—"

"But now you're an old married woman," Wilbur interrupted, "and have been for nearly three hours. Are you happy, my pet?"

Suzi looked across the room to see Harry returning from the small balcony overlooking the ocean, Mrs. O'Reilly on his arm. He was being kind to the housekeeper, because it was in his nature to be kind. It had also been in his nature, at the conclusion of the ceremony, to kiss his new bride until her toes curled inside her new white satin shoes. "Oh, yes, Wilbur. I'm happy. I'm probably also certifiably *nuts*. But I'm happy."

"Good," Wilbur said decisively, then struck when she was least suspecting an attack. "Now, why don't you be a good little girl and tell me who Harry really is."

Suzi's blood ran cold, something she had formerly imagined only happened in bad novels. Toying with the handle of her coffee cup, she mumbled, "Who is he? He's Harry Wilde, an Englishman I met here in Ocean City. I don't know what you mean."

"Never mind," Wilbur assured her smoothly, too smoothly, motioning for the waitress to bring the check. "I shouldn't have asked. Shall we head back to your condo for a few minutes? Then I shall have to be on my way. There's another art exhibit I have promised to attend this evening in the Village—a boring but necessary chore."

Suzi looked at Wilbur from beneath her eyelashes. "You aren't going straight back?" she asked, a sinking feeling in her stomach telling her that her old friend wasn't finished asking questions. He was just going to interrogate someone else. Someone like Harry.

It was nearly six o'clock before Wilbur's limousine backed out of the driveway with Wilbur and Mrs. O'Reilly inside. Wilbur had suggested that he transport the housekeeper back to Suzi's Manhattan condo, leaving the newlyweds on their own for a short honeymoon before they, too, returned to the city.

Suzi watched the limousine pulling away, fighting the urge to run after it and drag Mrs. O'Reilly back.

How could Wilbur have done this to her? He knew her quick marriage to Harry was due to strange circumstance, knew there was something strange about Harry himself. Wilbur knew everything.

So why had he abandoned her and taken her comfortable, live-in chaperone along as well?

"Hungry?" Harry asked, slipping an arm around her waist and guiding her back to the condo. "Mrs. O'Reilly said she left a meal for us in the refrigerator. Or would you rather walk down to the boardwalk and nibble on some pizza? Of course we'd have to change first. As you've said so many times, the best way to elude unwanted attention is to blend with the crowd."

Suzi sensed Harry's nervousness, and the realization comforted her. And then she was struck by inspiration. A terribly romantic inspiration, at least to her mind. "Harry, take off your jacket and tie," she said suddenly, pulling him into the foyer.

"Well, that's true enough, Suzi. There is a third alternative." His one-sided smile as he quickly stripped off his suit coat nearly caused her to race for her bedroom, bolting the door behind her.

"That's not what I meant!" she hastened to explain as Harry expertly worked the knot out of his tie and slowly slid the tie from beneath his collar. "I just thought we could walk on the beach, that's all. I've always wanted to walk on the beach in a long gown, the hem hovering just above the water as if I couldn't care less about getting it wet.''

"Ah, yes," Harry said, laying the jacket and tie over the banister. "I've seen the commercial on your television, I believe. The man and woman walk hand in hand along the water's edge as the sun goes down, the two of them barefoot—the man's trousers rolled up to his knees—as someone I can't see talks about stocks and bonds and preparing for something he called 'golden years.' Or perhaps the sun is rising? Do you think that matters?''

"No, Harry. It doesn't matter." Suzi thought she'd die of embarrassment. "Never mind. It was a lousy idea, and the dry cleaning bills would be sky high." She turned to go into her bedroom but he stopped her by placing his hand on her arm.

"No, dear heart," he contradicted, his voice low and faintly husky. "I believe it to be a sterling idea, truly. Just give me a minute to roll up my trousers and we'll be on our way."

She watched as Harry sat on the stairs and removed his shoes and socks. She had to swallow down hard on a rapidly rising excitement as he rolled up his pant legs to just below his knees, exposing tanned, golden hair-dusted calves, then stood and unbuttoned the top two buttons of his snowy white shirt. His hair had come free from the thin black ribbon he'd used to secure it at his nape and he used both hands to sweep it back from his face.

Damn the man anyway! If he got any more gorgeous he'd be declared illegal in all fifty states.

"Just a minute!" she said excitedly, racing to her bedroom to strip off her panty hose. There was nothing very romantic about walking in the ocean unless her legs were bare. She hesitated a moment before rejoining Harry, taking time to pick up her straw bonnet and take it along with her, holding it by its trailing satin ribbons. All the best romantic scenes included a large straw hat being carried by the beautiful heroine.

She would have checked her appearance in the mirror over her dresser, except that she was sure that if she did she would immediately remember that she was *not* a sweet, young, romantic heroine but nothing more than an over-thirty spinster who had hooked a husband only because he didn't have any other choice.

"Here I am," she called breathlessly as she stepped outside the condo to see Harry standing at the edge of the path, his fists on his hips, the breeze off the ocean ruffling both his long blond hair and the rolled-up sleeves of his dress shirt. She was struck by how much he suddenly resembled the man she had rescued on the beach, then shook her head, banishing the thought. Harry Wilde was no longer a stranger on the beach. He was her husband.

And she was scared to death!

Harry held out his hand to her and she took it, keeping her gaze directed toward the ground as they made their way across the wide stretch of sun-kissed sand and headed south along the shore, away from the boardwalk.

The beach was nearly deserted at this time of day, with the vacationers who rented the beachfront condos either eating their evening meal or dressing for a night on the boardwalk. In fact, except for a few die-hard body surfers and an elderly couple using metal detectors to sweep the sand for lost coins and jewelry, Suzi and Harry had the beach to themselves.

Neither of them spoke for at least five minutes as gulls screamed above their heads, the two of them concentrating on the scenery, their feet surefootedly finding the hard, cool, wet sand as wavelets curled around their ankles.

Then one larger, unexpected wave broke closer to shore and Suzi got her wish—her hem was suddenly soaked! "Oh, Harry, look what I've done!" she called out in disgust, shaking her hand free of his and running back up the beach a few paces, her hem clinging to her shins. "It's ruined. How could I have been so stupid?

"Nonsense, dear heart," Harry told her, pulling her back into the shallow water. "I find it most becoming. All the most daring young debutantes in Mayfair dampen their muslins."

Suzi felt a bubble of laughter rising in her throat as her jangled nerves calmed under Harry's sweet good humor. "They did, did they? And did all the most daring young bucks go wading with their trousers rolled up to their knees?"

"Our breeches were already *at* our knees, if you'll remember my water-soaked state when we first met," Harry reminded her, nudging her deeper into the water. "And I haven't been a 'young buck' in some years. I am—was—a Corinthian, a lover of sport and good wine, and beautiful women. Of course that is all behind me now."

"Because you hit your head, fell overboard and ended up in the twentieth century," Suzi said, her heart aching for him.

"No, dear heart," he answered, bending down to splash a fine spray of seawater on her skirt. "Because I am now a married man with sober responsibilities. I imagine I shall have to confine myself to watching sports, like Charlie, the clerk's lucky ex-husband, and concentrate on weightier matters."

Suzi ran a few paces ahead of him, then turned to hold up her skirts and kick a small fountain of water in his direction. "What sort of weightier matters would those be, good sir?" she asked, feeling suddenly carefree and, strangely, most remarkably beautiful. There *was* something to be said for walking along the ocean in a long gown, a large straw bonnet hanging from her arm by its satin strings, her hair free of its pins and curling about her face thanks to a gentle sea breeze.

Harry scratched at a spot behind his left ear as he grinned at her. "Allow me a moment to refine on that, sweet lady. I suppose," he said, taking her hand and turning her back in the direction they had come, "that I should concentrate on securing a comfortable future for my wife—that would be you. Strange, isn't it, how we, too, are speaking of 'golden' futures, just like the commercial? And then, of course, I shall have to go about setting up my nursery," he ended, pulling on her hand so that she had no choice but to follow him into the waves that now reached their knees.

His nursery? Suddenly Suzi was all out of snappy patter, her usually agile tongue cleaving to the roof of her very dry mouth. It was only when the next wave to hit the beach broke against her thighs that she shrieked and asked, "Harry, are you trying to drown me?"

He scooped her up in his arms at once, holding her high against his chest, the skirt of her gown plastered against her legs, clinging to the fabric of his pant legs. "Never, dear heart," he said, his expression so serious, his gaze so intent on her face, that she realized she was dangerously close to tears. "I'd never want to lose you. I was merely attempting to cool my ardor, for I know I should be hanged for what I'm thinking at the moment, husband or no husband."

"Oh, Harry." She laid her head against his broad chest, sighing, as he carried her back up the beach to the condo.

To the condo. To her empty condo. To her empty bed.

"You're not supposed to think, Harry," she said at last, daring to stroke his cheek with the back of her hand, daring to press a kiss against the intriguing hollow at the base of his throat. "Neither one of us is supposed to think. If we did, we would be left with no other choice but to run, screaming, into the sea."

Chapter Eight

Moonlight streamed in between the slats of the vertical blinds, spilling onto the bed. Patchwork, who had been spending her nights on Harry's bed, had taken up a place at the foot of the mattress and was curled into a small ball, sound asleep and contentedly purring.

Suzi's blond hair was spread fanlike around her head as she slept on her side, the sheet covering her to her hips, her right arm flung across Harry's waist.

As for Harry, he was propped against the pillows he'd pushed against the headboard, still awake, and caught somewhere between the greatest happiness and the most profound sadness he'd ever known.

He hadn't been the first, just as there had been women for him before Suzi. That was all right. He had been in twentieth-century America long enough to know that Suzi could not have been a virgin in this modern society unless she had been living alone on a mountaintop for the past thirty-two years.

Her lack of virginity didn't bother him; nor did her stammered explanation of a "stupid mistake" she had made in her mid-twenties, believing herself to be in love with a man when she had only longed to be in love.

What saddened Harry was the thought that he had missed being with Suzi for all of those thirty-two years.

He had missed her at the age of five, when all the world was a wonder.

He had not been privileged to know her at eighteen, with the world before her.

He had not been there to hold her hand, comfort her, be strong for her, when the world of her dreams and the world of reality had combined in her early twenties, when her parents had died and she had been forced to face that world alone.

But now he was here, and that was what filled his entire being with happiness, a golden glow of contentment, a fierce devotion, a vow to himself and to Suzi that she would never be alone again.

He looked down at her sleeping form, adoring the way her long lashes cast small shadows against her cheeks, the way she seemed to smile in her dreams. She was a marvel. Soft one moment, shy and deliciously nervous, responsive and burning with desire the next.

All her passion for living, all her endless enchantment with the world had centered on him as he had carried her in from the beach, laid her down on the bed, then joined her as he took that first, sweet kiss from her sea-kissed mouth.

His hands had trembled as they sought her, found her, molded her slimness, her sweet valleys, her soft, mounded curves.

And then the fire. The sweet fire. The all-consuming blaze that had simmered between them for so long had exploded in a white-hot heat that had left them both breathless, in awe, and unable to speak.

He closed his eyes, taking a deep breath, wondering what he had done to be so blessed, wondering when he would summon the nerve to do more than love her—to tell her how much he loved her. To put into words all that he had tried to say with his hands... his lips... his worshiping body...

"Harry?"

He looked down at Suzi, to see her in the process of tugging the sheet up over her bare breasts. "Yes, dear heart?" he asked, running a finger down over her nose, then playfully rubbing her soft bottom lip. "Have you wakened to realize that we have somehow neglected to partake of our evening meal?"

"Partake of our evening meal? Ah, Harry, how I love it when you talk Regency." She held his hand in place and began nibbling on the tip of his finger with her small, white teeth. "Is that what I'm feeling, Harry?" she questioned him, gazing up at him teasingly with those great, blue eyes. "Hunger?"

"Wretch!" he exclaimed, sinking fully down onto the mattress and taking hold of her, rolling her over on top of him. "You know, of course, that you are an extremely forward little minx?"

Her smile dazzled him. "Would you have me any other way, good sir?"

He threaded a hand through the silky hair at her nape, pulling her toward him. "I'd have you any way I could get you, madam," he admitted, reveling in the feel of her bare breasts against his chest, unsurprised by his quick arousal. "For the moment, however, and for the next fifty years or more, I'd much prefer having you just this way, in just this place."

She pressed quick kisses against the side of his throat, her fingers splayed against his chest, burrowing in the golden hairs she had only recently told him fascinated her beyond all reason. "Hmm, how nice. Please, sir, tell me more. I'm all ears."

"No, you're not," he told her, sliding his hands along her back, to the curve of her small waist, then lower. Deliciously lower. "Although they are most attractive, your ears, dear heart, are definitely not your most appealing feature. This, for instance, is very nice," he went on, curving his hands against her buttocks, then smoothing one hand upward to cup one perfect breast, "and I believe I have developed a definite preference for many of your other feminine attributes."

"Ah, more Regency talk. So formal, yet so deliciously sexy! More, Harry. Tell me more," she teased, her own hands becoming busy as she levered her body slightly to his right, exposing him to any liberty she might wish to take.

She took several, with both his unspoken agreement and his eventual breathless encouragement, before he rolled her over onto her back and straddled her. His kisses were hot and insistent, his heart pounding as he both felt the moment and anticipated the next moment, until he could stand it no more and took her, took himself, on their second journey in as many hours to the special heaven made for lovers.

And then they slept in each other's arms, this loving couple, without ever speaking a single word of love.

For now, for the moment, for this first night, words didn't seem to matter.

But what would happen, Harry asked himself as he finally drifted off to sleep, if all they would ever have were moments? What if he had come into Suzi's life for some sort of cosmic "moment" and could just as easily and unexpectedly fade out of it again?

"It's Yorkshire pudding."

Suzi watched as Harry eyed the concoction suspiciously. "Uh-huh," he said, obviously trying very hard not to laugh at her latest culinary effort. "Of course it is, dear heart. I should have recognized it at once—if it weren't so very, um, *fluid.*"

She allowed the pan to drop a full two inches onto the ceramic tabletop. "It's not just fluid, Harry. It's *liquid.*" She took off her oven mitt and threw it in his general direction, then returned to the stove and the cookbook that lay open on the counter. "Two eggs?" she read aloud, trying to refresh her memory. "Did it. One cup milk? Yup. We're all right so far. Two cups flour? *Two?* Does that say *two?*"

"Do I detect a hint of surprise in your voice, dear heart?" Harry asked, coming up behind her and slipping his arms around her waist as he laid his chin on her shoulder and peered at the page in the cookbook.

"Oh, put a sock in it, Harry," Suzi ordered, bending her knees so that she could slip out from under his chin, disconcerted by his closeness. They had been married for nearly two weeks, had made love every morning and evening ever since, but she was still as skittish as a young colt whenever Harry indulged in any friendly closeness. It was silly of her, darn near stupid, but she couldn't help it. They were great in bed. That didn't make them great anywhere else.

Maybe she was just trying too hard. Experimenting with recipes, trying to impress him with her domestic skills—a nonexistent talent to this point in her life—hoping to show herself as the perfect wife. It wasn't like her to play pretend, at least not with something so very *real,* and she should have given up the ghost on the project days ago, when she had accidentally broiled that chocolate cake.

She busied herself carrying the prime roast of beef into the dining room, secretly pleased that it smelled and looked heavenly, and called for Harry to join her.

He pushed the pan of ruined pudding to one side and held out her chair, once more complimenting her on the table decorations as he took his own seat.

"The centerpiece was a gift from Mrs. O'Connell next door. A wedding present. She gave it to me this afternoon," she said as she affectionately eyed the small piece of driftwood decorated with pink plastic flowers, the names Suzi and Harry having been spelled out along the base in seashell chips. "I think I know now how my dad felt every Father's Day when I handed him another tie I'd picked out myself. Poor Mrs. O'Connell. She means well. But you know something, Harry? I wouldn't sell that centerpiece for a million dollars!''

Harry laid a slice of beef on a plate and held it out to Suzi. ''One Christmas when I was nine or ten I presented my father with a rack for his pipes, a truly homely trifle that I'd stuck together from odd pieces of metal the smithy allowed me to work on at the forge. Papa always treasured it, as we shall treasure Mrs. O'Connell's gift. I hope you enjoy your beef rare, dear heart.''

Suzi sat up very straight and eyed the beef over the rim of the plate. She liked her prime rib rare. To her, it was the only way to eat it, and she often ordered the dish at *Charlie O's* before going to the theater. ''Oh, Lord, and it looked so good on the outside, too,'' she said miserably, slumping back down in her chair. ''That's not rare, Harry. That's raw. I'm surprised it didn't *moo* at you when you sliced into it.''

''I know a simple remedy for our dilemma.'' Harry picked up the platter and disappeared into the kitchen. A few moments later Suzi heard the oven door open and close. Then Harry returned to the dining room and stood behind her, to help her from her chair. ''I suggest we find something else to occupy us while the oven does its magic. It's all but impossible to ruin a good joint of beef, dear heart. We need only to be patient.''

She looked over her shoulder at him. ''Doesn't anything get you rattled, Harry?'' she asked, fighting back tears of frustration. ''I mean, isn't it boring being so damned British all the time? That stiff upper lip thing only works for so long, especially when you're hungry. You and that patience of yours could starve to death before your incompetent wife learns how to cook."

She stood and he pushed in the chair, then turned to smile at her. "I didn't marry you for your domestic prowess, dear heart. You possess other skills much more to my liking."

Suzi picked up the bowl of crushed corn and the dish of salad and headed for the kitchen to put them away, feeling her cheeks beginning to flush. That was the first time he'd even obliquely referred to their stunning compatibility in the bedroom *outside* of that bedroom, and he was making her nervous again, damn him.

"Maybe I could take another stab at making some Yorkshire pudding while we're waiting?" she suggested, her throat tight.

"Or we could take a walk on the beach, I suppose," Harry said, bringing in the single nearly raw slice of beef that he'd already carved and adding it to the roasting pan already in the oven. "Although Mrs. O'Connell says the neighbors on the other side of our condo have complained to her that they don't entirely appreciate hearing giggles coming from the beach at midnight."

"It isn't midnight, Harry," Suzi said, trying to tell him that he was crossing a line she didn't want breached. Their lovemaking was not to be spoken of, to her mind, not when so much of their lives remained unsettled.

Didn't he remember why they had married in the first place? Didn't he remember that they weren't just another married couple enjoying their honeymoon, but two near strangers indulging in a mad, impulsive adventure that could end badly?

Or didn't he see what she saw? Perhaps he didn't. And she wasn't about to discuss it with him. She refused to worry him about her anxiety late at night as he slept beside her, the nagging fear that was with her all day and that turned to stark terror in those long, dark hours after midnight.

The fear that she might wake up one morning to find him gone, returned to his own time.

"I think a walk on the beach would be wonderful," she said at last as he waited for her to answer, carefully pinning a smile on her face. "You see, I didn't want to say anything to you, but I think we should leave for Manhattan tomorrow. Other than the fact that I miss Mrs. O'Reilly's cooking, I really do have to go in to the office, deliver my reviews and pick up some more galleys."

She glanced up at him and winced inwardly, for he looked so solemn. She would have thought he could read her mind and knew how frightened she was. Or was he disappointed that she had all but slapped his face for speaking of their lovemaking? "Harry? Is something wrong?"

"Not a thing, dear heart," he said, his handsome face splitting in a grin. "I can hardly wait to see Manhattan. To take a bite out of the Big Apple. To walk along the Great White Way—Broadway. To visit Times Square, which sounds much like Piccadilly

Circus was in my day. And Wilbur has already promised to take me on an extensive tour of Langley Publishing."

Suzi was pleasantly surprised with Harry's ready agreement to their move to her New York condo—right up until the moment he'd mentioned Wilbur's name. That's when she began to smell a rat. "When did Wilbur invite you to Langley Publishing?"

Now it seemed to be Harry's turn to avoid *her* eyes. "I'm not completely sure. He could have issued the invitation shortly after he asked me if he could take the portions of my manuscript that I'd already transcribed back to Manhattan with him."

Suzi thought her eyes were about to pop out of her head. "He took the—you *gave* him the—and *I* haven't even been allowed to *look* at it? I knew it that day! Oh, yes, I knew. I could smell that he was up to something. That miserable little *sneak!* Turn my back for one minute, one *single* minute, and he—*damn,* you, Harry Wilde!" She gave him a swat somewhere in the vicinity of his left shoulder. "How *could* you?"

"I do so adore it when you become incomprehensible," Harry said, ruffling her hair before taking hold of her hand and leading her toward the spiral staircase.

She used her free hand to slap him on the back. "Never mind that now, Harry. Why did you give him your manuscript?"

"He asked," Harry told her with maddening calm. "If you had asked, I would have given it to you. You didn't. Wilbur did. It's that simple."

"Harry, *nothing* Wilbur does is 'simple.' Not *ever!*"
Suzi informed him tightly as she nearly stumbled on
the curving staircase. "But he doesn't fool me. Not for
a moment. He's looking for clues, the *sneak!*"

Harry stopped at the bottom of the steps and turned
to take hold of Suzi's waist as she stood on the second step. "Clues? Clues to what, dear heart? You may
say that I watch entirely too much television, but it
seems to me that you're the one who's sounding like
an installment of that show on lawyers I enjoy on
Thursday nights."

Suzi bobbed her head several times—rather in the
way of a person doing her best to hold on to her temper until the other person would shut up and she could
have her say. "Oh, yeah? Oh, yeah?" she bit out the
words sarcastically. "Well, a fat lot you know, Harry
Wilde. The day we got married, while you were ro-
mancing Mrs. O'Reilly out on the restaurant balcony,
Wilbur was asking me who you are. Who you really
are. Did you catch that, Harry? Wilbur wanted to
know who you *really* are. *Now* what do you have to
say for yourself?"

Harry was quiet for some moments, remembering
Wilbur's questioning glance when Harry had stumbled and referred to his trousers as breeches, then
sighed. "First, I should like to offer you my apolo-
gies. Secondly, dear heart, I'd say that tomorrow
might not be soon enough for us to travel to Manhattan."

If Ocean City had surprised and delighted Harry, his
initial look at the island of Manhattan had transported him to ecstasy.

Nothing he had seen prepared him for his first sight of the metropolitan skyline as viewed from the front passenger seat of Suzi's car. He didn't know where to look first, and he asked questions of Suzi, then barely waited for her answers before pointing in another direction to demand she tell him what he was seeing now.

But the ride through the long, white-tiled tunnel threaded deep beneath the river silenced him as he sat in awe of this feat of engineering, Suzi's explanation that a similar tunnel was being constructed to link England with France almost more than he could comprehend.

For centuries, England's safety had been measured in the miles of stormy channel water between itself and Britain's on-again, off-again enemies on the continent. Why would Britain ever want to militarily compromise itself in such a way?

He asked Suzi, who answered simply, "With today's missiles and jets and smart bombs, Harry, it doesn't matter anymore that the English Channel is even there. Besides, England and France have been allies for years and years. Now, don't ask any more questions for a while, Harry, okay? If you thought the New Jersey Turnpike was bad, you ain't seen nothing yet! I've got to concentrate on getting us through this traffic in one piece."

He obeyed easily, for he was struck speechless as he held on to his seat with both hands, watching bug-eyed as Suzi threaded her car into narrow streets clogged with cars, and trucks, and taxicabs, and people walking straight into the flow of traffic seemingly without looking, without caring that they were making a bad situation worse.

The narrow streets were lined on both sides with structures taller than he had ever seen except for St. Paul's Cathedral towers—some of the structures appearing to be made entirely of glass, some of them so old and black with soot that they had lost any beauty they once must have had. It was as if the buildings had blotted out the sun, and the world was reduced to this single street and its hulking buildings.

And then there were the signs. Huge, garish advertisements of every vice known to man—and several rather bizarre entertainments Harry considered to be beyond the realm of possibility.

People of all colors and persuasion crowded the sidewalks.

There were men dressed in everything from sober business suits to casual clothing such as Harry had observed on the Ocean City boardwalk, to decrepit creatures who appeared to be wearing everything they owned, none of it worth a bent penny.

He saw women in skirts so short and shoe heels so high that both seemed painful to wear, others clad in summery dresses, and still others wearing what appeared to be gentlemen's suits, only the bottom half of their legs were bare.

And everyone he saw was obviously in a great hurry to reach their destination.

The cacophony of blowing horns, and screeching brakes, and high-pitched screams, which Suzi told him were sirens, and hawkers crying their wares, and even one man haranguing a crowd of people stopped at one corner, warning them that doom was at hand, melded together into one, great racket, so that Harry was at last forced to raise the window to shut out the heat and the dust and the noise.

"Suzi?" he asked, not knowing whether to be impressed or disgusted. "Is all of Manhattan like this?"

"Not all of it, Harry," Suzi answered, pointing to her left. "See, down this street? And over there?" She pointed to her right, nearly poking him in the nose. "We're in the theater district now. In a dozen or so more blocks we'll be out of the worst of it. Hey!" she yelled, jamming her foot on the brake while pressing on the disk at the center of the steering wheel, so that Harry heard a horn blowing very close to his own ears as he held on to the dashboard, in fear of his life. "Where'd you get your license, buster? Mail order? Did you see that, Harry? That idiot cut me off!"

"Suzanne," Harry said tightly once they were on their way again. "Now that I'm, as you refer to my status, *legal,* would it be possible for me to learn to navigate an automobile?"

She sliced him a quick look from behind her huge, bright red-rimmed sunglasses before pulling around a large truck loaded to the gills with garbage. "I suppose so. Why do you ask?"

He scratched at a spot behind his left ear. "Because, dear heart, much as I admire your courage and determination, I do not believe I will be able to continue sitting idly by in this seat while allowing you to take my life in your hands."

"Is that your stuck-up way of inferring that you don't approve of the way I drive?"

"Why, yes, dear heart," he answered, grinning. "I do believe it is. I am the man in this small family of ours and, speaking both for myself and for Patchwork—" he glanced into the back seat to see the calico cat cowering inside her small plastic wired cage "—I must say that I would feel much more comfortable with the reins—that is, the *wheel*—in my hand."

"You didn't complain when we were in Ocean City," Suzi said, her lower lip stuck out, her pout adorable, Harry thought.

"And I once allowed a young lady—her brother was a notable whip and had taught her how to tool the ribbons—to drive my curricle in Hyde Park for the Promenade. That does not, however, mean that I was so paper-skulled as to trust her to thread her way down Bond Street at noon," Harry pointed out, he thought, reasonably.

Suzi frowned for a moment more, then grinned at him. "Don't worry about it, Harry. I don't drive in Manhattan. A person would have to be certifiable to do this every day—which explains a lot of our cabdrivers, I suppose. I drive into and out of Manhattan, on my way to New Jersey or to visit my friends Daniel and Joey Quinn in Pennsylvania, but I don't drive in the city. For the most part, all this car does is collect dust and ridiculously high parking garage fees. Happy now?"

"Momentarily mollified, Suzi," Harry corrected before once more becoming interested in the changing scenery outside the car. The street were wider now, and less crowded with trucks, and there were even small islands of green to be seen here and there. The garish signs were gone, and he felt as if he had just driven from Piccadilly into the comfortable neighborhoods of town houses and stately mansions known as Mayfair.

"Good Lord, what's that?" he asked, pointing to his left once more. "I know you don't have royalty here in America, but that building could do competition with Prinny's Carleton House."

"That, Harry," Suzi informed him, "is the New York Metropolitan Museum of Art, better known as the Met. And stop talking about America as if you're just a visitor. As far as anyone except Wilbur is concerned, you were *born* here, remember? Okay, here we are—home sweet home," she said, pulling the car over against the curb and stopping. "You can help Fred, he's the doorman, with our luggage, and then Fred will deliver my car to the parking garage."

Harry opened the passenger door and went to assist Suzi from her seat, only to jump back quickly as one of the yellow taxicabs blew by him, horn blaring. This Manhattan was going to take some getting used to, he decided, prudently retreating toward the curb as the independent Suzi maneuvered herself past the gearshift and climbed out onto the sidewalk.

"Are you all right, sir?" a man in an elaborate uniform asked, taking his arm. "Gotta watch it around here, you know. Those cabs fly past here trying to make the turn and pick up fares at the Met. Gotta keep your eyes open every minute, isn't that right, Miss Harper?"

"Absolutely, Fred," Suzi said, looking at Harry as if to inspect him for injuries. She then introduced him to the doorman, whom Harry had for a moment believed to be a member of the military. He held out his hand to Fred, who hesitated for a second, looking both surprised and flattered by the gesture, before his face split in a grin as he shook Harry's hand.

"So our little Miss Harper is married?" Fred exclaimed, beaming as he energetically pumped Harry's arm up and down. "Well, that's something Mr. Langley didn't tell me when he and the lady arrived a little while ago and Mrs. O'Reilly buzzed him on through."

Suzi and Harry exchanged quick glances, Suzi saying, "I phoned Mrs. O'Reilly yesterday to tell her we were coming. Damn it, Harry, I'm going to make that man make my quarterly payment for her withholding tax, considering that she's as much in his employ as she is in mine. Come on. Grab a couple of suitcases and let's get this over with!"

"Fred said Wilbur had a woman with him," Harry said, following after Suzi.

"Yeah, he did, didn't he," Suzi shot back, her blue eyes glittering. "And I'll bet my single Picasso sketch that the woman's name is Courtney Blackmun. I'm thirty-two years old. Isn't it time everyone stopped treating me as if I couldn't find my own way out of Bloomie's?"

"I'm sure Wilbur is simply concerned—" Harry began before Suzi cut him off.

"Concerned? Get real! *Nosey* is what I'd call it! Damn, Harry, I love my friends, but there are days—"

"Is something wrong, Miss Harper—er, that is, Mrs., Mrs.—gosh, I forgot!"

"Wilde," Harry reminded Fred proudly after opening the trunk and tossing the car key to the doorman. "Mrs. Harry Wilde. The name suits her down to the ground at the moment, don't you think? But don't worry, everything's fine."

He then pulled five heavy cases out of the trunk, watching as Suzi picked up two of them, then slammed the trunk, grabbed the three remaining cases and took off after his irate bride as she walked beneath the canopy, heading for the front door.

He wasn't accustomed to following where any female led, but in Suzi's case, and knowing that Wilbur was upstairs waiting for them, he didn't see that he had any other choice. Although Harry did take a moment to admire Suzi's legs as she glided along in her short skirt and delicate high-heeled shoes, believing that, if nothing else, the varied women's fashions of the twentieth century might make up just a little bit for the modern man's loss of superiority.

Not that he'd ever say as much to Suzi. She'd only give him another lecture on something she called "equal rights," then reel off a list of women who'd climbed mountains, fought in wars, become great judges and doctors and corporate presidents—and even flown into space, all while raising children, keeping a neat house and reminding their totally helpless husbands where they had left their car keys.

He entered the elevator behind Suzi, only his third elevator ride to date, so that he watched the buttons in admiration as he was lifted seemingly effortlessly to the eighth floor. He didn't have any other choice, actually, because Suzi was standing face front, her chin at a belligerent angle, almost as if *daring* him to say anything, just so she could tell him again, "I *told* you so!"

Chapter Nine

"Plague and Pestilence? Oh, no, Suzi. Don't tell me Sydney's been using her pet names for her brothers in public. The twins are fine, believe it or not. They're still at computer camp, driving their counselors wild, I suppose," Courtney Blackmun said as she sat at her ease on the long white couch in Suzi's living room.

Harry stood beside the small, portable bar, an untouched glass of wine in his hand, knowing himself to have been favorably impressed with the bestselling author the moment he first saw her as she came forward to wrap Suzi in an enthusiastic bear hug.

Courtney was a beautiful, sophisticated woman, one Harry could not believe to be the mother of a married daughter. And, of course, he liked her immediately because Courtney liked Suzi, and Harry would always like anyone who appreciated his very singular wife.

Not that Harry was at his ease, for Wilbur was also in the room, looking his usual elegant self, but with a sparkle in his eye that was most disconcerting.

While Suzi and Courtney chatted together, Suzi proudly showing off her wedding ring and regaling her friend with details of the marriage ceremony, Wilbur discreetly crooked a finger in Harry's direction, then disappeared into the kitchen.

Harry looked to Suzi, who was describing the trellis Wilbur had ordered installed in the living room of the hapless justice of the peace, and knew he would not get any help from her. She was deliberately ignoring him, wordlessly telling him that he was the one who had gotten them into this latest trouble by giving Wilbur the manuscript and he was darn well the one who would have to find a way to get them out again!

And she was right. Dealing with Wilbur Langley and the man's "inquiring mind" was his problem. Setting his glass of wine on the bar, he took a steadying breath, squared his shoulders and headed for the kitchen, feeling as if he were fourteen again and on his way to the headmaster's office to be read a lecture on the foolhardiness of keeping a monkey in his rooms.

"I've read your manuscript, my boy, and enjoyed it immensely," Wilbur said without preamble, which was the very last thing Harry had thought the man would say, and which was a move that put him totally off his guard.

Wilbur liked his work? He really liked it? Harry hadn't held out much hope in that quarter, firmly believing that his scribblings would not be attractive to anyone born after 1800.

"Really, Wilbur?" he asked, trying not to preen outwardly at the publisher's praise. "But you haven't seen more than a quarter of it—not that it's totally finished in any case. The section on my—that is, the character's varied adventures during his reluctant service during the War of 1812 is incomplete."

Good Lord! Why couldn't he guard his tongue? A few words of flattery and he was acting as if his brain was to let—a vain popinjay with no consideration for his safety, for the safety of Suzi and their shared secret.

Wilbur leaned a hip against the countertop, his fingers laced together in front of him. "Ah, Harry, that's true enough. But I've been in the business for a long time. I know brilliance when I see it. It's a fascinating coming-of-age story, only with a twist, that twist being that I haven't read anything so startlingly *real* in some time. Even your spelling—so imaginative, so much in the way of the period—is an added fillip."

Harry merely smiled politely, determined not to say anything else until he felt more sure of himself, or until Suzi rescued him, which he was fairly certain she would not do.

"You know," Wilbur went on, "I believe I would want to keep the spelling as it appears now, rather in the way Stephen King's publisher printed page after page of *Misery* as if it were a real, typewritten page from a manuscript. It was an ingenious if expensive device, complete with handwritten letters to make up for the character's supposed difficulty with a malfunctioning typewriter. Not that keeping the spelling will add to our costs, even if it will give our proofreaders fits. Yes, yes. That's settled. The spelling will remain as it is."

"You—you're going to publish my work?" So much for holding his tongue, Harry thought, knowing Wilbur was drawing him in, deliberately trying to gain his confidence. But the possibility of seeing his words in print was so heady, so intoxicating, that he longed to hear more.

"Publish it? Dear boy, I will *produce* it! I will tout it, push it, and then step back modestly and watch it climb to the heights of the bestseller's lists, where it will remain for a long, long time. Harry, dear man, you have succeeded in relating a most wondrous tale of a young Regency gentleman's journeys in the world. The work is not fanciful, like Byron's, but very real, and touching, and rather humorous as well—as well as curiously relevant to today's youth. I haven't read such disbelief dispelling fiction in twenty years!"

"Fiction?" Harry smiled, letting his pent-up breath out slowly. So he was wrong. Wilbur didn't suspect anything. "I've always enjoyed fiction, Wilbur," he said, relaxing. "Although I never thought to be compared with George. When I read his *Childe Harold's Pilgrimage* this past spring I was bowled over by its beauty, its power."

"Just this past spring, Harry? I would have thought Byron would be required reading in all English schools," Wilbur said, looking at him closely, so that Harry knew he had put his foot in it again.

"Oh, I read Byron in my youth, surely," he improvised quickly, "but not with any great relish. It is only now that I am older that I appreciate his brilliance in anything other than breaking female hearts. You know how it is with young lads, Wilbur."

"Vaguely. There are times I don't believe I ever was young. Then again," he added, smiling, "there are those who would say I never grew up at all. Very well," he added, pushing himself away from the counter. "We'll leave mundane things like contracts and advance payments until another time and rejoin the ladies before they take offense at our absence, but we do have an agreement, don't we?"

Harry couldn't believe it. He wanted to grab the publisher and kiss him on both cheeks. Not only was he now an American, but he was married to his adorable Suzi, and now he would be able to support her in the manner to which she was already accustomed! "You're really serious, Wilbur? You really want to publish my manuscript?"

Wilbur smiled and patted Harry on the shoulder. "I am always serious, Harry, when it comes to literary pursuits. Just ask Courtney if you don't believe me. Or my dear daughter-in-law, whose work mirrors your own, if in more modern terms. By the bye, Harry, is Byron half as handsome in life as he is depicted in his portraits?"

"Oh, yes. George is definitely most hand—" Harry said, then froze in the act of turning toward the living room. Suzi had been correct. Wilbur Langley was a *sneak.* "You *know,*" he accused, eyeing the publisher in trepidation. "Bloody hell, Wilbur—how long? How long have you known?"

"Since that first evening, I suspect," Wilbur answered coolly, although Harry noticed that the older man's usually pale white skin had gone rather gray, as if he had hoped he would not be proved correct. "I still don't quite believe it, but I've always known it."

"From Courtney's phone call?"

"You mean the one telling me that Suzi had rung her up in Japan in the middle of the night to share the harebrained scheme that she was going to write a time-travel novel and needed a way for her hero to gain legal identification? Yes, that did have something to do with raising my suspicions. Quite a bit to do with it, as a matter of fact. At first I thought she had become the dupe of an illegal alien wishing to use her to gain resident status in America, but after meeting you I began to consider something entirely different, although I decided to pretend I believed Suzi's explanation. Not that I'd even entertain such a farfetched notion as time travel if it had been anyone but Suzi. The most outlandish things do happen to that girl," he ended, shaking his head.

"And you're not upset?" Harry asked, looking into the living room to see that Suzi and Courtney were still deep in conversation, Courtney balancing a pile of manuscript pages on her lap. "You don't object? No," he then added consideringly, "you couldn't object, could you, my friend? Otherwise you wouldn't have helped us procure identification, and you most certainly wouldn't have given our marriage your blessing."

Wilbur gestured toward the living room with one well-manicured hand. "Look at her, my boy," he demanded imperiously. "Suzi is one of a kind, rather like you. And she is rapturous and even more beautiful than when I first met her nearly a decade ago. How can I object to anything—to anyone—who gives the dear girl such happiness? As her friend, as your friend, I would not do anything to hurt either of you."

He turned and looked at Harry, ending sincerely, "You may face an uncertain future, but if you love enough, any problem can be surmounted. All I ask is that you be good to her, my boy. For if you ever deliberately hurt her I shall be obliged to destroy you."

Harry extended his hand to the older man, his expression equally serious. "You have my word as an English gentleman, sir," he promised. "Suzi may not yet be aware of it, but I love her with all my heart. As you say, she is one of a kind. A most singular woman."

Wilbur smiled as if satisfied with Harry's answer, then abruptly changed the subject, as if he had said and heard all he wished to say and hear on the matter of Suzi's future.

"I'll want the journey through time put into your book. Not this one, but the next work of *fiction*. You see, I do plan for you to have a long, successful career, as do most all of Langley Publishing's discoveries. Not that you aren't good, and deserving of any success, but in a country that could make pet rocks a national phenomenon, it is not very difficult to promote an author to temporary fame and fortune with the right marketing plan. It is keeping himself popular for several decades that is the true test of the great writer. I believe you will pass that test."

"Thank you, Wilbur," Harry said, knowing he was beaming with pleasure at the man's kind words. What a wonderful place this America was—so different from the time and place he had come from! He had heard that America was the land of opportunity—or so many emigrants from Ireland and Northern England had thought in his day, but Wilbur's plans for him exceeded all his expectations, all his greatest hopes.

To write, to communicate what was in his mind, his heart, with others had been his dream since his late boyhood, even though his father had not been receptive to the plan. Neither had the few publishers he had contacted on Paternoster Row, for they were much more interested in fanciful, romantic tales such as those penned by Byron and Sir Walter Scott.

That was how he had come to be aboard the *Pegasus* in the first place, having succumbed to the notion that he could please his late father's soul by serving with the forces sent to America after his service with the army against Napoléon had been limited to those of one of Wellesley's many clerks, tucked safely away from the fighting and the glory and the adventure Harry's sire had deemed so necessary to the building of a young man's character.

Would his father be proud of him now, now that he had achieved a measure of "adventure" even his sire could never have dreamed possible? Now that he was on the threshold of "glory" thanks to the possibility of some success with his work?

Harry believed his father would be proud, if he could only know. And who was to say that he didn't know? After all, who would have said it was possible to travel through time? *Anything* was possible!

"Harry? Why are you standing there grinning like you just won the lottery?"

Harry blinked and shook his head, surprised to see that Wilbur had joined Courtney in the living room and Suzi was now standing beside him in the kitchen.

He smiled as he looked down at his wife, wondering if she knew how wonderful she was, how beautiful she would always be in his eyes, and how very much he loved her. But when he opened his mouth he heard himself say, "He knows."

"He? Wilbur? He knows? What does he know?" She placed a hand on his arm. "Harry, has the trip been too much for you? I know I'm not the best driver in the world, but I already told you I don't drive in Manhattan. And if you need to lie down or something I have to tell you that you don't have time for that right now. Something's happened, and I have to talk to you—just as soon as we can convince Courtney and Wilbur that we want to be alone."

Harry belatedly noticed that Suzi was looking a little pale, rather in the way Wilbur's complexion had whitened as he learned for certain that Harry had come to America from sometime in 1813. Something had happened in the living room, something between Suzi and Courtney. Did the bestselling author also suspect that Harry had traveled through time?

"He knows, Suzi," Harry repeated in a whisper, believing Suzi should learn all of the truth at once. That way, if she decided to faint with shock she would only have to swoon the once, and not again and again. "Wilbur knows I traveled here from Regency England."

Suzi looked into the living room, to where her two friends were gathering up their belongings in preparation of leaving, then glared up at her husband. "That's not funny, Harry," she whispered back fiercely.

"And I am not attempting to be amusing," Harry countered in a low voice, deciding that Courtney had not been made privy to Wilbur's suspicions before their visit. "He has suspected as much almost from the beginning, or so he said, but he tricked me into admitting the truth just a few minutes ago."

"*Tricked* you?" Suzi pulled him farther into the kitchen and repeated, her voice once more lowered, "Tricked you? Oh, really. And how did he do that, Harry? How did Wilbur *trick* you into spilling your guts about the most *important* secret you'll ever have to keep? Honestly, Harry, people say *women* can't keep a secret. Well, those people haven't met *you* then, have they? Luckily it's Wilbur. He wouldn't tell a soul, because he adores knowing something no one else knows, and because he knows I'll *pulverize* him if he so much as hints to anyone about how you got here. But do you know how lucky you are that it's only Wilbur? I mean, Harry, how could you have—"

"He bought my manuscript," Harry broke in, just to see if Suzi would react and because he didn't need any lectures from his wife when he already knew he had blundered, badly.

She didn't disappoint him. Her anger dissipated in a heartbeat and her features softened, her huge eyes glowing with pride. "He bought it? Wilbur bought it?

Oh, *Harry!*" she exclaimed, then went up on tiptoe to all but crush his neck in her exuberant embrace.

He slipped his arms around her waist, not so blockheaded as to ignore a chance to hold his wife, and caught her mouth with his own.

The explosion of passion he had come to associate with any intimate encounter with Suzi pulsed through his body and Harry further indulged himself by running his hands along his wife's spine, pulling her closer against him. All thoughts of his book, Wilbur's revelation, even the presence of Courtney Blackmun, fled his mind along with any remaining nineteenth-century notions of proper public behavior as Suzi melted against him.

It was only as he heard a door closing somewhere in the distance that he broke off the kiss and buried his mouth against Suzi's throat. "Might I surmise, dear heart," he asked in a low, amused purr, "that you are tolerably pleased by this news?"

She pushed herself away from him, placing her flattened palms against his chest. "Idiot! Of course I'm pleased. I'm more than pleased!"

"And, being pleased, your first instinct was to kiss me? I cannot tell you how gratifying that is, when I consider that the sun is still high in the sky and all forms of affection have to date been relegated to those hours between dusk and dawn."

"Harry," she answered, taking his hand, clearly having taken the bit between her teeth and anxious to run, "don't start. Not now. Besides, I kiss complete strangers when I'm happy—or I would, if I ever was happy enough and around a stranger at the same time.

Come on, I want to talk to Wilbur. I've never acted in the role of agent before, but I know how it goes, and you do need representation, even with Wilbur. Why, this may be the beginning of a whole new career for me—''

She stopped just inside the living room, frowning. ''They're gone!''

Harry pulled her close against his side. ''Yes, I thought I heard the door close a few moments ago. A discreet pair, Courtney and Wilbur. Either that or your very public display of affection embarrassed them.''

''Court and Wilbur embarrassed by a kiss? Get real,'' Suzi admonished, pulling him over to sit on the couch. ''Courtney was just being polite. And I'll bet you she had to drag Wilbur out of here. He always said he'd give several thousand dollars to see me in—''

She clapped her hands over her mouth, her eyes wide as saucers.

''To see you in what, Suzi? To see you in the institution of marriage? To see you kissing in the kitchen?'' Harry asked teasingly, moving close beside her on the couch, believing this to be a day made for revelations. ''Or, could it be something else? To see you in *love*, perhaps?''

She concentrated on the design in the Oriental carpet. ''I have a big mouth,'' she groused, then looked up at him. ''It seems we have more in common than we thought. Mr. and Mrs. Big Mouth, that's us.''

Harry felt his face splitting in an unholy grin and was slightly surprised his wife didn't hit him. "Then you do love me?" he asked, knowing the answer.

"All right. Yes. I love you. I don't know why, because there's no real reason I should, and you are the most infuriating mixture of Regency stuffiness and the worst of what you've learned watching that stupid television—but I do love you, Harry Wilde," Suzi said, her small body fairly shaking with fury. "Are you happy now?"

"Happy? Yes, I believe I am. Happy, elated, delighted, even overjoyed. Rapturous, actually," Harry said, tipping up her chin with his fingertips. "You see, dear heart, I quite adore you, and always will. You have the most generous, unselfish heart of any woman I ever met. You're never still for a moment, I never know what you're going to do next, and you're the most potentially *dangerous* cook in creation—but I love you Suzi Wilde."

"Oh, Harry!" Suzi exclaimed, throwing herself against him, so that he lost his balance and the two of them toppled back onto the cushions. "That was the most wonderful thing you've ever said to me!" And then, abruptly, she hopped to her feet, leaving him lying alone and disappointed on the couch. "However, we have a problem. We've had it all along, ever since the beginning—we even talked about it that first day— but now we have to *really* talk about it. Even if the subject scares me to death."

Harry shook his head, trying to clear it of thoughts of Suzi and the wide bed where he had only an hour earlier deposited their mountain of luggage. But he

had already admitted he never knew from one minute
to the next what Suzi would do, so he took a deep
breath, saying, "I'm at your service, dear heart. Now,
what is our new, yet old, problem? I feel able to solve
any difficulty at the moment."

"Well, good luck on this one." She picked up some
papers, those he remembered Courtney handling earlier. "It's in this, Harry," she said, waving the pages
in front of his nose. "You're not going to believe this,
Harry, but I've inspired Courtney! She brought this
along to show me—a copy of the working synopsis for
her next book."

"That's nice, Suzi," Harry answered, reaching into
his pocket for one of the slim cigars he had discovered at an Ocean City convenience store. Suzi's enthusiastic embrace had bent it nearly in half, but it was
still smokable, so he straightened it as best he could
and slipped it between his teeth. "Not as nice as nibbling on your ear while I carry you into the bedroom,
but nice. Go on."

"Don't be a spoilsport, Harry," Suzi warned, then
sighed dramatically. "She came to me for advice on
how to end the book, wondering if I had thought of
how sticky the ending could get. You see, this is only
a partial synopsis. Courtney hit what she thinks is a
roadblock to the happily ever after all romance novels require."

Striking a match, Harry took several quick puffs on
the bent cigar, then looked up at Suzi through a haze
of blue smoke. "And she came here today to ask you
to help her? I thought you said she was a bestselling
author. Why would she need your help, not that you

aren't brilliant? And adorable. And desirable. Not only that, but you love me. Are you quite sure you wouldn't want to go to bed?''

Suzi rolled her eyes. "I'm not getting this out right, am I? Hmm, I love the smell of a good cigar—and you look so sexy with it! Lord, I can't believe we just told each other that we love each other and now we're just sitting here, stuck in another problem. Just don't inhale, all right? Cigars aren't good for you."

"Neither is physical frustration, dear heart, I imagine, but you don't seem to be worrying overmuch about my health on that score," he pointed out, grinning around the cigar. He'd let her finish whatever it was she was trying to say, then toss her over his shoulder, if necessary, and adjourn to the bedroom. "But Courtney did want your input?"

But Suzi wasn't listening. She was rereading the last few pages of Courtney's notes again, and her expression was becoming more and more anxious. "Sort of, I suppose," she answered absently, "not that she wouldn't eventually think up something plausible for her made-up heroine, who traveled to Victorian England after slipping down a rabbit hole, sort of like *Alice in Wonderland,* but with a twist. That's the beauty of fiction. You can make up your own reality. Only we can't can we? Court was just talking, and probably wondering if I'd thought of the problem when I decided to write my own book, which I'm not going to write because you'll probably write it, which is fine with me, except if we don't solve this problem you might not write it after all. Harry, get the luggage. I'll ring for Fred to bring the car around, and then I'll explain as I drive. We're going back to Ocean City."

"The devil you say!" Now Harry leapt to his feet, snatching the pages from Suzi's hand, all thoughts of romance fleeing his mind as he mentally sorted through Suzi's delightful ramblings and realized that she was truly upset. "What's in here, anyway?" He scanned the pages quickly, glancing at his wife every few moments. "Courtney is writing a novel about a character that travels through time?"

Suzi was already busily scribbling a note to Mrs. O'Reilly, who was out shopping. "Yes, darn it all anyway. And I already told you that, or at least I think I did. She got the whole idea from me, actually, which should flatter me, which it doesn't. She said she knew darn full well I'd never *really* write a novel—and she's right, not that I appreciate her knowing me that well—so that I wouldn't mind if she tried her hand at one. They're very popular right now, you understand. Time-travel novels, that is."

Harry continued to read as he listened to Suzi's garbled explanation with one ear. "Go on. I've yet to see a problem."

"That's just because you didn't get to the last page. You see, Courtney realized that the reader had to be assured that whoever traveled through time was going to *stay* in the time he or she landed in, because otherwise there couldn't be any happily ever after."

She picked up her purse, laying the strap over her shoulder, then turned to Harry, her blue eyes glistening with unshed tears. "I thought I was the only one who had thought about that. About—" her voice broke for a moment "—about how long you might be here."

Harry closed his eyes for a moment, then crossed the room to take Suzi in his arms. "You're not the only one, dear heart," he told her, pressing her close against his chest, wishing he could think up something brilliant to say, something that would end her fears. "I've thought about it, too."

Suzi pushed him away, lifting her chin defiantly, as if deliberately deciding to be courageous. "I know. We did talk about it a little bit that first day, but it didn't seem to matter then. But it matters now. We didn't come to Manhattan because I had to get back to work. We came here because I thought taking you away from Ocean City, away from the place where you traveled through time, might keep me from losing you. Well, now that I know that's not going to work, I think the only thing we can do is go back. There's a local museum in Ocean City. If we can find something, some record from 1813 that mentions the *Pegasus* and what happened to it, maybe we'll discover the proof we need to believe that you're here for keeps."

"And if we don't?" Harry asked, already mentally agreeing to the drive back to Ocean City. "What then, dear heart?"

She gave him a watery smile. "Then, Harry," she told him, "I will just have to find a way to travel back in time with you. Because you're not going to get away from me, Harry Wilde. Not now that I know I couldn't possibly want to live without you."

Chapter Ten

The storm broke just as Suzi turned the car onto the Ninth Street Bridge leading onto the island, the twilight sky unnaturally dark this early in the evening.

Thunderstorms on the island were never placid affairs, with the breeze from the ocean stilling and a hot wind beginning to blow off the land just before the first violent streaks of lightning lit the sky.

Suzi remembered her first encounter with an Ocean City storm. She had been walking the boardwalk with a crowd of Fourth of July tourists when the air had stilled, then become warm as the wind shifted. A murmur went through the crowd, those vacationers and natives who knew what was going to happen already taking their children's hands and heading down the boardwalk in either direction, intent on finding one of the ramps that led to the street.

Suzi had stood at the railing, still nibbling on a cardboard stick twirled around with fluffy pink cotton candy, watching the people—novices like herself, she'd later realized—watching the sky.

And then the breeze had accelerated into a wet wind, heavy raindrops pelting the boardwalk, lashing the people who were now all running down the length of the boardwalk, Suzi among them.

Thunder rolled, lightning cracked and the rain was so heavy she might as well have been running in a swimming pool, for she was that wet. The cotton candy congealed on the stick, turning into a hard, dark pink blob, so that she tossed it away in the nearest trash can at one side of the boardwalk, then shielded her eyes with her hand as she looked back at the crowd behind her.

It was a scene out of a Saturday-afternoon matinee from her checkered youth, Suzi had decided, watching as hundreds of people loaded with jackets and baby strollers and bags holding purchases made at the boardwalk shops ran past her, some of them loudly calling to their children to hurry, all of them taking time to glance behind them as the storm pressed down on the shore. If *Godzilla* had suddenly appeared beyond the tall streetlights positioned on the beach side of the boardwalk Suzi wouldn't have been a bit surprised.

This, she knew, was one of those violent, invigorating, vaguely frightening summer storms.

Very much like the one that had brought her Harry Wilde.

Would this one take him away again?

Was Harry thinking what she was thinking? That she had brought him back to Ocean City just in time for fate to take him away from her?

"Can you see to navigate, dear heart?" Harry asked as he used a paper napkin to wipe the steamed-up windows. "Perhaps it might be wise if you pulled over now that we're across the bridge and wait for the storm to abate a little? Damn it all, Suzi, I feel so useless!"

Suzi shook her head, battling the rain that made her windshield wipers almost useless, wishing the defroster could better clear the windshield of the fog their combined breaths had caused, narrowing her eyes to squint through the unnatural darkness and find the signpost that marked Wesley Avenue. "We have to get home, Harry. I have to get you inside, away from the storm."

"I don't melt in a little rain, dear heart," he assured her, patting her arm.

She shot him an angry look, then silently berated herself for believing, if only for a moment, that he wasn't aware of what she was thinking.

She gripped the steering wheel tightly with both hands. It wasn't fair. It wasn't fair! She had waited thirty-two years to find her love, and now she might lose him!

She turned the car into the short driveway in front of her condo and they both ran for the safety of the overhang above the front door, hesitating only as Suzi searched her key ring for the correct key. "Damn, damn, *damn!*" she muttered as the ring fell from her hands, sobbing now in her terror.

Harry bent to retrieve the keys then, instead of opening the door, took her hand and led her along the path leading to the beach.

"What are you doing? Are you nuts?" she called to him above a loud clap of thunder. "The beach is the last place you want to be at a time like this."

She kicked off her high-heeled pumps before they were pulled off by the deep, sucking sand, then tripped up the outside stairs to the deck, Harry still in the lead and holding her hand. He pulled her down onto her knees on the rain-lashed wooden boards, facing him, the three-foot-high walls of the deck doing little to protect them from the wind and rain.

He held her against him tightly, their bodies pressed together from knee to chest. Then he cupped her face between his hands, and looked deeply into her eyes, his handsome, deadly serious face lit by another wild streak of lightning. "Did you really mean it, dear heart? If a storm brought me to you, and a storm will take me away, do you really mean to go with me? Do you love me that much?"

"Yes!" Suzi cried, finding it difficult to see him in the darkness, holding on to him so tightly she could barely tell where her body left off and his began. They were one person now. Now and forever. She would never let him go. "Oh, yes, darling. *Yes!*"

And then, still holding her, he slanted his mouth against hers as they fell back against the wooden deck floor, the wrath of the storm and their combined fears and deep love for each other only adding to the fury of the night as they dedicated themselves to each other with their words, their hearts, their very souls.

She kissed his rain-wet body, molded his hard muscles beneath her fingers, strained with him and against him as sodden clothes disappeared and they dared the elements with their nakedness, their passion.

Suzi had never felt so alive, so elementally female, so free to express her desires and likewise free to accept anything Harry might ask of her.

Their coming together was fierce, raw and fraught with tension, fraught with a fury that matched that of the storm raging all around them.

And when it was over, as the thunder faded into the distance and the lightning died, leaving behind only a watery moon and gentle, blessing rain, they lay contented on the wooden deck, together and, at least for this one night, this one storm—triumphant.

Harry didn't know why he felt drawn back to the small, overrun cemetery where they had discovered the headstone of William Robert Arthur, but early the next morning he insisted that Suzi drive them there so that he could have another look around.

As he had told Suzi, not without pain, the fact that they had survived one storm together did not necessarily mean that they had found a way to accomplish a happily-ever-after ending to their worries.

Last night's storm had not been the same as the one that had brought him into Suzi's life. There had been no "eye," no instant calming of the storm. In fact, it was still gray and drizzling as Suzi turned the car into the graveyard and switched off the engine.

"I think William Robert's grave is over there," she said, pointing to a row of headstones that was the last before the cemetery seemed to deteriorate into several rows of considerably older stones. "That is what you wanted to see, isn't it?"

Harry took her hand as they exited the car and began picking their way through the puddles in the rutted gravel driveway. "I'm not sure," he admitted, feeling once more the eerie sense of déjà vu that he had experienced upon his first visit to this cemetery.

At the time, he had thought it only meant that this would be the cemetery where he would discover his new identity, and had not mentioned his reactions to Suzi. But now—well, there was something, some nebulous something, that had drawn him back, was still drawing him, so that he continued to walk, not sure of his destination but confident he would find something.

And there it was, in the last row of the cemetery.

A thin headstone sunk almost sideways in the sandy ground, nearly submerged in shore grasses that waved to him in the breeze.

He dropped to his knees in front of the stone, his fingers nearly numb as he parted the grasses in order to read the faded inscription, "Here lie the earthly remains of Harry Wilde, an English sailor presumed lost from the warship *Pegasus* and washed ashore, drowned, 4 August 1813. Interred in this place through the sweet charity of the Daughters of the Revolution."

"My God, Harry—you did drown!"

He glanced up at Suzi, who was looking at him as if she'd just seen a ghost. A ghost? Was he a ghost? He didn't feel like a ghost. He didn't even believe in ghosts. Of course, he hadn't believed in time travel until a few weeks ago, either.

"I don't know," he said quietly, still staring at his headstone. It was very queer, looking down at his own headstone, reading about his own death. Not the sort of thing to cheer a man, to be plain about the thing. "What do you think, dear heart?"

"I think," she said, tugging at him so that he was forced to stand, "that it's time we acted on *my* idea. It's time we played the tourists and took a tour of Ocean City's historical museum. Come on, darling."

Neither of them spoke on their way back to the island, although Harry was convinced Suzi's mind was as crowded with questions and suppositions as his, none of them comforting. It was only as they had parked the car and were walking toward the small building containing artifacts of Ocean City's history that Harry dared to put one of these thoughts into words. "Can ghosts father children?" he asked, taking Suzi's hand in his.

"You're not a ghost, Harry!" Suzi all but shouted at him. "My life may be bizarre, but I refuse to believe I married a ghost. Time travel I can live with. It's off the wall, but somehow explainable—sort of. But a ghost? That's going too far, Harry, even for me."

Harry nodded, accepting Suzi's logic, not as if he had a multitude of choices. He could be a figment of Suzi's imagination—or Suzi and her world a figment of his—or he was a ghost, or he had left his mortal body, traveled through time with a new body, and might just take another flit in the next storm. No. There wasn't a whacking great lot to choose from.

"Scared?" he asked Suzi as he stepped forward to open the door to the museum.

"Petrified," she admitted, then smiled at him, so that he knew that, no matter what they found inside the museum, he had already discovered everything in the world that meant anything to him.

The museum was interesting, or would have been if Harry could only relax as he walked through rooms filled with relics of Ocean City's past, including some of the salvage from the wreck of the *Sinda,* a merchant ship that had long ago come to grief off the shore of the island.

"There's nothing here from the *Pegasus,*" he remarked to Suzi, who had become interested in a display of china dolls and other toys she said had been popular when her mother had been a girl.

"The *Pegasus?*" a pleasant-faced older woman repeated as she laid down her knitting, left her chair at the side of the room and walked toward them, patting at her gray bun that was slipping badly. "Now why does that name seem familiar to me? Hello, folks. Are you enjoying your stay in Ocean City?"

"Very much," Harry answered, bowing to the woman who reminded him very much of his childhood nanny, who was forever knitting something, although she never seemed to finish any of it. "I am a teacher," he lied easily, because it had always been easy to fib to his nanny, who had constantly amazed him with her easy credulity, "and I have been instructing my students in the War of 1812. There was an English ship during that war—the *Pegasus*—and it supposedly sailed the waters just off Ocean City. As my wife and I are visiting your city on our vacation, I thought—"

The woman slapped her forehead, as if that might jolt her memory. "Of course!" she exclaimed happily, looking to Suzi. "That's where I heard the name. That's where poor old Harry hailed from—the *Pegasus!*"

"Poor old Harry?" Suzi questioned, and Harry could tell by her tone that she was amused to hear him spoken of in such an easy, familiar way. "Oh, please, I must hear more about poor old Harry!"

The woman clasped her hands together in front of her and began, "Well, as I remember hearing it, there was a terrible storm at sea, and on the island as well, and the *Pegasus* was caught in it. It didn't come to grief, the way the *Sinda* did, but one of its sailors was apparently washed overboard and drowned. His body was found on the beach, somewhere up around the Twenty-eighth Street beach, I believe. Of course it wasn't the Twenty-eighth Street beach then, but just a stretch of sand, for the island was barely populated."

Harry and Suzi exchanged bemused, expectant glances. Suzi's beachfront condo was located on Wesley Avenue, just at Twenty-eighth Street. "Go on, please," Harry said, his heart pounding as he listened to the woman tell him about his own death.

"There isn't too much more to say, actually," the woman said, shaking her head. "There was a collection made by the good women of the area and the man was buried on the mainland—I don't recall which cemetery—and that was the end of it. Except for the pouch, of course. That's here."

"My—the pouch?" How could his pouch be here, in this museum? His pouch was packed in his luggage and safely locked up in Suzi's condo. "What sort of pouch, ma'am?"

The woman turned, motioning for Harry and Suzi to follow her into the next room, and Suzi took his hand, squeezing it comfortingly.

"It's just a pouch. You know, a purse? A knapsack?" the woman offered, standing just inside the door, her hands on her hips as she surveyed the crowded room. "Poor old Harry was wearing it when he washed ashore. It probably would have been a good idea to take it off so that it wouldn't weigh him down, but then I remember reading that lots of sailors couldn't swim a lick in those days, so maybe it wouldn't have mattered anyway. Now where is it?"

"The pouch was heavy?" Suzi asked, walking around the perimeter of the room, scanning the shelves for the pouch. "Was there something in it?"

"Yes, yes," the woman answered distractedly, still searching the shelves with her anxious gaze. "There was some gold coin, a packet containing the man's identifying papers—that's how we know he was poor old Harry—and another thick bunch of papers written all over in some sort of code. The seawater had made a muck of most of it, but I remember someone telling me that even what they could read didn't make a lick of sense. Now where is it hiding? Honestly, ever since we moved here from our old quarters I've been searching for things that were misplaced. But I could have sworn I've seen that pouch right in this room. It was just there on the second shelf, right where that empty space is, but now it's gone. Now, why would anyone want to steal poor old Harry's pouch?''

Harry smiled at Suzi, sure she was thinking what he was thinking. No one had stolen the pouch. No one had because it belonged to him, was precious to him, and he had somehow retrieved the pouch and brought it with him through time, a kindly nature or heavenly intervention reversing the death he had supposedly died one hundred and eighty-one years previously.

His grave would be empty now, too. He would be willing to wager his last gold coin on it!

He had always been meant to survive his fall overboard, because he had always been meant to meet Suzi Harper and fall in love. He had always believed he would meet a woman he could love. He just hadn't thought it would take him one hundred and eighty-one years to accomplish the feat!

The woman turned to them, spreading her hands apologetically. "I'm so sorry. Either I'm wrong about seeing it here, and the pouch was lost in the move, or it was stolen. Not that it matters, for sure as I'm standing here someone will hear about it and make up some fanciful story—like all the other stories about poor old Harry.''

"Other stories?'' Harry repeated as Suzi came to stand beside him. ''I don't understand.''

The woman gave a wave of her hand. "Oh, there's a million of them around here. Why, you can buy books on all our New Jersey ghost stories at most any shop on the boardwalk. Poor old Harry's just one of them. Let me see, how does it go? Oh, I know!''

Harry could feel Suzi's excitement as she stood beside him, fairly dancing in her anxiety to hear what the woman had to say.

''Well,'' the woman said consideringly, walking with them back toward the entrance, ''it seems that, as far as the story about poor old Harry goes, he appears on the beach just before dawn every August fourth—that's the day he was found, you understand. If you were to get up very early, and look very hard, you can see him lying there, just at the water's edge, suspended between life and death, waiting for someone to come save him.

''Only there's a hitch, of course,'' she went on as Harry tried to concentrate upon remembering to breathe. ''By the time anyone who sees him can get to him, poor old Harry's gone. Poof! Disappeared into the early-morning mist.''

She smiled as she held open the door, allowing in the bright sunlight that had at last broken through the clouds, just in the way the storm pelting the *Pegasus* had stopped and the sun had come out over the ocean.

''You know, it's a pity the story isn't true,'' the woman said, sighing in the way of a young, romantic girl. ''Just think how lovely it would be to rescue poor old Harry from his watery grave. Ah, well, it's just one of those old legends, isn't it? We have a million of them! But it is odd about that pouch. Very odd.''

''Odd?'' Suzi exclaimed, grabbing the woman and kissing her on both cheeks. ''It's not odd at all—it's *wonderful!* Thank heaven for Mrs. O'Connell and her driftwood! And thank you, you sweet, adorable woman. Thank you *so much!* Come on, Harry, we're going home!''

"Harry?" the woman questioned, her voice little more than a squeak, looking back and forth between Harry and Suzi. "That would be a coincidence, wouldn't it?" she asked, smiling weakly and she looked around behind her for a chair.

"Absolutely, madam," Harry told her joyfully, also kissing her on both cheeks. Suzi had been right—if she were ever happy enough, and in the company of a stranger, she would kiss that stranger, and just had. Harry felt the same way. He wanted to kiss everyone in the whole, entire, wonderful world!

But, mostly, he wanted to kiss Suzi. He wanted to kiss her, and hold her, and thank her for rescuing him from the limbo he had unknowingly inhabited for the past one hundred and eighty-one years, waiting for a stubborn, headstrong, singular woman like Suzi Harper to come along and defy the fates by snatching him from that limbo and taking him into her life, her heart.

"Wilbur was right, dear heart," he told Suzi as he led her back to the car at a near run. "I'm going to be a very good writer. After all, I have such intriguing stories to tell! But first, I believe I am going to spend several uninterrupted days and nights with my bride."

"Oh, Harry," Suzi said, pushing him back against the front fender of the car and sliding her arms up and around his neck. "It's unbelievable. We've done it, haven't we? We've found our 'happily ever after.' I love you, Harry Wilde. I love you so much!"

"That's good, dear heart," he told her as he lowered his head to hers, his gaze intent on her smiling mouth, "because you're going to have me around for a long, long time."

Epilogue

The seventh annual Wilde beach party, slated each year for the fourth of August, was in full swing.

Senator Adam Richardson, whose twins, Pete and Paul, were now in their second year of college, had flown in from Washington during the Senate recess to be with his wife, Courtney, who still returned to Ocean City each summer to work on her yearly novel. *Twice Upon A Time,* her bestselling time-travel romance, had been such a hit five years ago that she had finally agreed to do a sequel. More than once she had walked up the beach to confer with Harry, who was always pleased to give her the benefit of his own "research" into the subject that had landed his second book, also a time-travel novel, on the *Times* list for over a year.

While Adam modestly accepted Daniel Quinn's congratulations on being named to the Judiciary Committee, Daniel's father-in-law, Wilbur Langley, sat on the deck with Joey, Daniel's wife, discussing his planned redecoration of his Ocean City condo. Wilbur was always redecorating something, and this year the condo had been on his list, and Joey was trying not to smile as Wilbur discussed the Early Egyptian motif he was considering.

Rick, Daniel's son by his first wife—Wilbur's deceased daughter—was also on the deck. He had just finished his first year of residency at the Hospital of the University of Pennsylvania and was now playing a board game with his young sisters and brother, and losing badly.

That left Sydney and Blake Mansfield, who were still down on the beach with their twin girls and their infant son, who had been born just this past spring. Sydney was lying in the sun, her long, slim body already a golden tan, while Blake was allowing himself to be buried by the giggling twins, who considered this attack on their father to be a yearly ritual.

Mrs. O'Reilly stepped out onto the deck, her hands full, holding a tray of freshly cut up fruit, and nearly tripped over William Wilde—the "great" Billy Wilde, as the blond, blue-eyed youngster preferred to be called—who was lying on his belly, tickling the feet of his baby sister, Elizabeth, who was cooing in her infant seat.

"Billy, my boy, you'd be better served to take yourself down onto the beach with your brother Robbie rather than to lie about like a beached whale. He's helping to bury your Uncle Blake at the moment," Harry advised, kissing his wife's hand as she passed by him to pick up their daughter. Robert, aged three, was the blondest of the three children, his hair so fair it was almost white, and both boys were already showing signs of being as tall as their father.

"Oh, I don't know," Suzi said, winking at her husband. "You never know what might happen to you if you just 'lie about like a beached whale,' Billy. Why, you might even discover your own true love."

"Yech! Mom, that's *gross!*" Billy exclaimed in the disgust only a six-year-old could feel about the subject of true love. "Sorry, Mrs. O! I didn't mean to trip you," he hastily apologized to the housekeeper, then scrambled to his feet to thread his way through the mass of deck chairs filled with the people he had come to know as his extended family and raced down the steps to the beach.

Suzi deposited Elizabeth in her doting father's lap and collapsed into the chair beside Harry, smiling in real contentment. "It never rains on August 4 anymore, does it, darling? We've had brilliant sunshine every year for our party." She leaned close to him, whispering, "This is the one day of the year Wilbur finds himself frustrated. He's the only one who knows why August 4 is important to us, and he can't tell anyone. He must feel as if he could burst!"

Harry kissed his daughter's turned-up nose, then repeated the gesture with his wife. "Wilbur would never burst, dear heart. It might ruin the line of his suit. Although he did seem to puff up a bit with pride as he told me about the advance sales on my latest book."

"Don't brag, darling, it isn't polite," Suzi warned, ruffling his long blond hair, which she had adamantly refused to allow him to cut more in the fashion of the day. "But, if you can blow your own horn, I imagine I can tell you that I made the cupcakes this year. All by myself, too. Mrs. O'Reilly didn't even help."

Harry rested his forehead against his daughter's and told the child confidentially, "Yes, my little namesake of her esteemed Royal Highness, I know. I saw the boxes from the bakery, too. But I won't tell if you don't."

"Harry Wilde!" Suzi exclaimed, giving him a playful tap on the shoulder. "You weren't supposed to know."

"Know what?" Courtney asked, pulling up a chair and sitting down beside them. "Never mind," she added, sighing. "It's a lovely day, isn't it? I never tire of Ocean City."

"Neither do we," Harry said, taking hold of his wife's hand and bringing it to his lips. "It's a very special place. Almost magical, isn't it, dear heart?"

"Harry," Suzi said warningly, and then she smiled, because Harry was right. Ocean City had been magical, for Courtney, for Sydney, and just seven wonderful years ago, for her.

And she wouldn't have believed any of it, if it had happened to anyone else but her.

*　*　*　*　*

JINGLE BELLS, WEDDING BELLS:
Silhouette's Christmas Collection for 1994

Christmas Wish List

*To beat the crowds at the malls and get the perfect present for *everyone,* even that snoopy Mrs. Smith next door!

*To get through the holiday parties without running my panty hose.

*To bake cookies, decorate the house and serve the perfect Christmas dinner—just like the women in all those magazines.

*To sit down, curl up and read my Silhouette Christmas stories!

Join *New York Times* bestselling author Nora Roberts, along with popular writers Barbara Boswell, Myrna Temte and Elizabeth August, as we celebrate the joys of Christmas—and the magic of marriage—with

JINGLE BELLS, WEDDING BELLS

Silhouette's Christmas Collection for 1994.

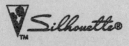

JBWB

MILLION DOLLAR SWEEPSTAKES (III)

No purchase necessary. To enter, follow the directions published. Method of entry may vary. For eligibility, entries must be received no later than March 31, 1996. No liability is assumed for printing errors, lost, late or misdirected entries. Odds of winning are determined by the number of eligible entries distributed and received. Prizewinners will be determined no later than June 30, 1996.

Sweepstakes open to residents of the U.S. (except Puerto Rico), Canada, Europe and Taiwan who are 18 years of age or older. All applicable laws and regulations apply. Sweepstakes offer void wherever prohibited by law. Values of all prizes are in U.S. currency. This sweepstakes is presented by Torstar Corp., its subsidiaries and affiliates, in conjunction with book, merchandise and/or product offerings. For a copy of the Official Rules send a self-addressed, stamped envelope (WA residents need not affix return postage) to: MILLION DOLLAR SWEEPSTAKES (III) Rules, P.O. Box 4573, Blair, NE 68009, USA.

EXTRA BONUS PRIZE DRAWING

No purchase necessary. The Extra Bonus Prize will be awarded in a random drawing to be conducted no later than 5/30/96 from among all entries received. To qualify, entries must be received by 3/31/96 and comply with published directions. Drawing open to residents of the U.S. (except Puerto Rico), Canada, Europe and Taiwan who are 18 years of age or older. All applicable laws and regulations apply; offer void wherever prohibited by law. Odds of winning are dependent upon number of eligible entries received. Prize is valued in U.S. currency. The offer is presented by Torstar Corp., its subsidiaries and affiliates in conjunction with book, merchandise and/or product offering. For a copy of the Official Rules governing this sweepstakes, send a self-addressed, stamped envelope (WA residents need not affix return postage) to: Extra Bonus Prize Drawing Rules, P.O. Box 4590, Blair, NE 68009, USA.

SWP-S994

Dark secrets, dangerous desire...

Lovers
DARK AND
DANGEROUS

Three spine-tingling tales from the dark side of love.

This October, enter the world of shadowy romance as Silhouette presents the third in their annual tradition of thrilling love stories and chilling story lines. Written by three of Silhouette's top names:

LINDSAY McKENNA
LEE KARR
RACHEL LEE

Haunting a store near you this October.

Only from **Silhouette®**

...where passion lives.

MIRA™

The brightest star in women's fiction!

This October, reach for the stars and watch all your dreams come true with **MIRA BOOKS.**

HEATHER GRAHAM POZZESSERE
Slow Burn in October
An enthralling tale of murder and passion set against the dark and glittering world of Miami.

SANDRA BROWN
The Devil's Own in November
She made a deal with the devil...but she didn't bargain on losing her heart.

BARBARA BRETTON
Tomorrow & Always in November
Unlikely lovers from very different worlds... They had to cross time to find one another.

PENNY JORDAN
For Better For Worse in December
Three couples, three dreams—can they rekindle the love and passion that first brought them together?

The sky has no limit with **MIRA BOOKS.**

**HE'S MORE THAN A MAN,
HE'S ONE OF OUR**

**DAD ON THE JOB
Linda Varner**

Single dad Ethan Cooper didn't have time for women. But he needed
Nicole Winter's business to get his new company going. Then he saw
his latest client play mother to his two kids and he wanted her for so
much more....

Dad on the Job is the first book in Linda Varner's **MR. RIGHT, INC.,**
a heartwarming new series about three hardworking bachelors in the
building trade who find love at first sight—construction site, that is!
Beginning in October.

Fall in love with our Fabulous Fathers!

Silhouette
R O M A N C E™

FF1094

Silhouette

SPECIAL EDITION

WILD RIVER

Maddening men…winsome women…and the untamed land
they live in—all add up to love!

A RIVER TO CROSS (SE #910)
Laurie Paige

Sheriff Shane Macklin knew there was more to "town outsider"
Tina Henderson than met the eye. What he saw was a generous
and selfless woman whose true colors held the promise of love….

Don't miss the latest Rogue River tale, A RIVER TO CROSS, available
in September from Silhouette Special Edition!

BABY'S CHOICE

Join Marie Ferrarella—and not one, but two, beautiful babies—as her "Baby's Choice" series concludes in October with *BABY TIMES TWO* (SR #1037)

She hadn't thought about Chase Randolph in ages, yet now Gina Delmonico couldn't get her ex-husband out of her mind. Then fate intervened, forcing them together again. Chase, too, seemed to remember their all-too-brief marriage—especially the honeymoon. And before long, these predestined parents discovered the happiness—and the family—that had always been meant to be.

It's "Baby's Choice" when angelic babies-in-waiting select their own delivery dates, only in

V *Silhouette* ROMANCE™

To order your copy of *Baby Times Two*, or the first two "Baby's Choice" titles—*Caution: Baby Ahead* (SR #1007) and *Mother on the Wing* (SR #1026)—please send your name, address, zip or postal code, along with a check or money order (please do not send cash) for $2.75 for each book ordered ($3.25 in Canada), plus 75¢ postage and handling ($1.00 in Canada), payable to Silhouette Books, to:

In the U.S.
Silhouette Books
3010 Walden Ave.
P. O. Box 9077
Buffalo, NY 14269-9077

In Canada
Silhouette Books
P. O. Box 636
Fort Erie, Ontario
L2A 5X3

*Please specify book title(s), line and number with your order.
Canadian residents add applicable federal and provincial taxes.

SRMF3